Witness Before the Fact

E. X. FERRARS

G.K.HALL & CO.

Boston, Massachusetts

1980

Library of Congress Cataloging in Publication Data

Ferrars, E   X
    Witness before the fact.

    Large print ed.
    1. Large type books. I. Title.
[PR6003.R458W5 1980]   823'.912   80-23874
ISBN 0-8161-3126-0

All of the characters in this book are fictitious, and
any resemblance to actual persons, living or dead, is
purely coincidental.

Published in Large Print by arrangement with
Doubleday & Company, Inc.

Set in Compugraphic 18 pt English Times by
Cheryl Yodlin

Witness Before
the Fact

CHAPTER 1

When the telephone rang at Peter Corey's elbow, he knew that it would be Clare. She had a habit of telephoning about nine o'clock in the evening, just when he had settled down to watch the news. He had to switch the television off before he could answer.

When he said, "Hallo," she said, "Peter?" just as if it might possibly have been someone else. Tonight this irritated him and he wondered, as he often had before, why he had spent so much of his life in love with someone who had so many irritating little habits.

But the irritation did not sound in his voice as he said in his stolid way, "Yes,

1

Clare. How are things coming along?"

He had the manner and the appearance, if not the feelings, of a very stolid man, solemn, unemotional, a bit slow. He was forty-five and looked more because his brown hair had thinned above his forehead, leaving it high and bare, and his thickset body had recently been putting on some extra weight. He was vaguely concerned about this, though not enough to cut down on his whisky or consider drastic changes in his diet and he went on taking the same amount of exercise as before, a walk of about two miles, when he had finished his day's work, through the quieter side streets of Kensington.

His height was five foot ten, but only when he pulled himself upright. Usually he had a slightly slouching way of standing which made him seem squatter than he was. His eyes were grey, good-natured, and more observant than they seemed. He had very little interest in clothes and usually dressed in conservative grey suits, of which he had accumulated a fair number in recent times, but which were all almost identical.

Clare Methven answered him, "I've finished the drawings, Peter. I'm pleased with them. I think you will be too. Suppose you come round for lunch tomorrow and take a look at them."

"Thank you, I'd like to do that. When shall I come?" he asked.

"Oh, come early. Twelve o'clock. Actually there's something I'd like to talk over with you, apart from the drawings. Just an idea I had, but it's rather important to me. Incidentally, how's the idea for the new book coming along? Are you going to have some more work for me soon?"

"I don't think so. I don't seem to be getting anywhere," he said. "As a matter of fact, I've been thinking of taking a holiday."

"That's what you said last time we talked. Have you made any plans?"

"Not really."

"It's a long time since you've gone away anywhere. I often think you're getting too settled down. Well, I'll see you tomorrow at twelve."

"Thank you."

Now what does she want of me, Peter wondered as he put the telephone down, switched on the television again, and picked up his glass of whisky. When Clare had something that she specially wanted to discuss with him it generally turned out that she had some request in store, something that he, and only he, could do for her. And he invariably agreed to do whatever she wanted, if it was in the least practical, which it sometimes was not. She had some curious ideas about his capabilities. But the thought of disappointing her scared him acutely. His hold on her was so tenuous that he had only to fail her a few times, he thought, and he would lose her completely.

Not that that would necessarily be a bad thing, except that it would upset his work. He would have to find a new illustrator. And since he did not know for certain whether it was his stories or her illustrations that made the Edward Otter books sell so well, he might find, if he finally broke with her, that he had landed himself in some serious difficulties.

Edward Otter had been their joint

creation, born long ago when Peter had still been a lecturer in the Department of English in the University of Hong Kong and Clare had been the wife of Alec Methven, inspector in the Hong Kong police. The first book had been produced more or less as a joke, to pass the time, and Peter had never known just why he had decided to write about a kingdom of otters, for he had known almost nothing about them and had still come face to face with one only in the Regent's Park Zoo. But Edward Otter, defender of the peaceful otters against the fierce, invading, imperialist mink, had sprung into Peter's mind, complete with his eccentricities, his shy heroism, and his quiet guile, as if he and Edward had always known one another.

Clare, in her illustrations, had seemed to have an immediate understanding of him too. Then the book had sold far beyond their expectations, so it had been only natural to write another, and now, with one coming out each year in time for Christmas and Edward Otter toys in the shops and a television series that seemed to be going on forever, they were providing both Peter and Clare with comfortable incomes, so that Peter had been able to give up his university post and Clare to leave her husband without either of them feeling the pinch of financial anxiety.

Peter wasn't sure whether Clare would have left Alec if she had not stumbled on a pleasant way of making an independent income. Alec's pay had not been high and even if he had been generous when they separated, any allowance that he might have been able to make her would not have kept her in the style that she enjoyed. She had seemed careless of money at the time, but Peter had come to realise that in fact she was shrewd and cautious.

But perhaps that had only developed as she grew older. The breakup had happened a long time ago, more than fifteen years. She was forty now, which was a difficult thing to remember since she always looked so young, but Peter knew that she herself was very conscious of her age and afraid of it and of the passing of time.

He arrived at her flat in Hampstead next day punctually at twelve o'clock. It was near Swiss Cottage in a block built fairly recently in a street where the earlier Victorian houses had been demolished, and had a lift and a porter and an atmosphere of moderate luxury. The flat was on the fifth floor, with a fine spread of sky to be seen from the windows, but the rooms were small and too crowded with furniture, books, pictures, and oddments of glass and china to be anything but rather a mess. Clare was a compulsive buyer of odds and ends. Even the room where she did most of her work was crowded with knickknacks, most of them charming and a few of them valuable, though scattered around in such profusion that it puzzled Peter how she managed to keep them clean. But this she scrupulously did. She was very fastidious and after her own fashion surprisingly tidy. Every object had its proper place and she would have noticed it at once if any of them had been moved.

When he rang her bell at the entrance to the block of flats, her buzzer sounded and he pushed the door open, went to the lift, and pressed the button for the fifth floor. She was waiting in her open doorway by the time that he reached it. She slid her arms round his neck and kissed him on the mouth, one of her quick, friendly kisses, which was all that he expected from her now. Kissing him at all, he knew, was just a habit and he half-wished that she would give it up. But making an issue of it had never seemed worthwhile.

"A drink first," she said as she led him into her small, cluttered sitting room, "then I'll show you the drawings. I do think they're good, Peter. I think they're about the best I've done."

She went to a tray of drinks that had been put down on the open flap of a Georgian bureau among heaps of letters, bills, bank statements, sketches, and notebooks. At first glance these appeared to be in total disorder, but Peter knew that Clare would have been able to put her hand on any one that she happened to want without having to search for a moment.

Pouring out whisky and soda for him,

as he liked it, and sherry for herself, she sat down on a small, high-backed Victorian sofa and swung her feet up on to it. She was a small woman and slender, but with rounded hips curving below a waist which in spite of her age was tiny. Her hair was very fair and fine, looped down softly on each side of her face. It was a puckish face, with high arched eyebrows and an upturned nose and eyes of a very pale blue that had a deceptive, mild, unfocussed look about them. Deceptive because they often looked as if she were not attending to you at all and was lost in some private dream when in fact she was a very good listener with an almost uncanny memory of anything that had been said to her. Today she was wearing jeans, a plain white shirt and sandals, and no ornament but a silver ring set with a big white topaz.

"Well, sit down," she said, "and tell me about this holiday of yours."

Peter sat down on a curiously shaped chair, one of the few modern objects in the room, which tilted back startlingly as he sat in it. The first time that he had done so he had thought that he was about to fall over backwards, but by now he knew its tricks.

"I told you, I haven't got very far with planning anything," he said.

"That's fine, that's just fine, because that's what I want to talk to you about. The trouble is, you're going to think I'm crazy." She gave him a smile which lit up her face for a moment, but which faded quickly, leaving her looking unusually unsure of herself, as if she were really a little afraid of what he might think of her. "I told you I'd had an idea, didn't I? It's about Alec. I don't know why, but recently I've found I keep thinking about him. Not worrying exactly, but feeling there's something I ought to be doing about him. And so I've been wondering, if you're thinking of taking a holiday, if you'd consider visiting him? You always liked each other, didn't you?"

Peter was more than a little startled. Clare very seldom spoke of her husband, though Peter knew that she had never entirely lost touch with him. She always seemed to know where Alec was and what

10

he was doing. Peter could not remember any occasion when she had said that she had had a letter from him, yet it seemed that they must write to one another occasionally.

"Yes, of course I always liked him," he said, "but we haven't had any contact for years. I don't see how I could possibly descend on him all of a sudden."

"But he'd love it!" she exclaimed. "I know he would. You were one of the few people he honestly liked. He didn't like many people, you know. That was one of the things about him I found so difficult, because he didn't want me to like them either and normally I like people rather indiscriminately, and need them too. Well, you know all that about me. But he really did like you and actually listened to what you had to say."

"That kind of thing can change in fifteen years."

"No, it doesn't. What happens to you as you get older is that your old friends mean more than ever to you, because you find it harder and harder to make new ones."

"Are you forgetting that I stole his wife?"

"For which he was grateful."

"But if he wanted me to visit him, he could have written to me himself."

"Yes, but you know what he's like. He'd never do that. He doesn't expect people to care about him."

"And do you care? Why, so suddenly?"

She gave another of her quick smiles that faded almost at once, leaving her looking graver than before. "I always have, you know. I never stopped being fond of him. But now I'm puzzled and worried."

Peter knew that she had never got Alec wholly out of her system. During the brief time when she and Peter had been lovers he had thought that she had been half-regretting the breakup of her marriage. Certainly he himself had never been able to give her whatever it was that she had wanted. Making love had released a curious streak of aggression in her. At the time it could seem to be all that she desired, yet afterwards, only too often, it was followed by outbursts of petulance,

12

recrimination, even tears. After a little while he had begun to wonder if she ever really enjoyed it at all, or if she was forcing herself simply as a way of getting even with Alec. She had had to have a lover in order not to be a failure, and Peter had been there. It had been a peculiarly unhappy time and a relief, though he had not realized it at first, when it had ended.

But because of Edward Otter, the tie between them had never been wholly broken. That well-meaning animal, who had always been deeply anxious not to do any harm to anybody, not even his enemy, the mink, who was to be won over to his way of thinking by persuasion, not by violence, had been largely responsible later for the failure of Peter's marriage. From the very beginning, Margaret had been deeply jealous of Clare. It had been a complicated sort of jealousy, not all simply sexual, but based as much on the fact that she and Peter shared something in which Margaret could have no part, as on the fact that they had once been lovers.

To make matters worse, she had realised

that in a sense she was dependent on Clare. Edward Otter was her creation as much as Peter's and it was Edward Otter who had provided Margaret with her comfortable way of life. The marriage had lasted three years, then she had left for Canada with a young doctor who had been hoping to earn more money than he could make in Britain. And Clare had still been there at Peter's elbow, affectionate as always, loyal to him after her fashion, only not in love with him.

That he had never quite been able to get over being in love with her sometimes made him bitterly angry with himself. He derided his feeling for her by calling it a fixation. Whatever it was, it had brought about the failure of other love affairs even more easily than that of his marriage to Margaret. Sometimes he wondered if he hated Clare. But as hate can be as obsessive an emotion as love, what did it matter what he called it? Whenever she wanted something of him, he did his best to provide it. He knew that he would give in now over this curious desire that she had that he should visit Alec.

But first he wanted to know a little more about it. That was really necessary.

"What is it exactly that's worrying you about him?" he asked. "You must have some idea."

"Well, money, for one thing," she said. "There he is, living on Madeira, which isn't the cheapest place in the world, and where's his income coming from? He's never told me much about that kind of thing since he left the police and went off to the Congo, but in the last letter I had from him he said something about giving English lessons to waiters and taxi drivers, which doesn't sound like affluence. And if things are too bleak, I could help him a bit. I hate to think that he might actually be in want."

"How long ago did this letter about the taxi drivers come?"

"It wasn't exactly a letter, it was a Christmas card with some oddments of news scribbled into it."

Christmas, and it was now May. It had taken Clare a fair time to start worrying about her husband.

"You could go yourself and find out

how things are," Peter suggested.

"Oh, he'd never let that on to me, he's much too proud," she said. "But he might tell you the truth."

He gave her a thoughtful look, so small, so pretty, so concerned.

"What are you really after, Clare?" he asked. "You aren't wondering, are you, about giving marriage a second try?"

"That would be absurd, of course," she said. "I could hardly expect him to be interested, could I, even if I thought . . . No, no." She laughed. "Once was enough for me. Marriage isn't my thing. I'm not asking you to go out there as a matchmaker, Peter. I just want to know how he is, for old times' sake. Is that really so abnormal?"

"A bit, I think," Peter said. "But I'll tell you what I'll do. Give me his address and I'll write to him and say that I'm thinking of a holiday on Madeira and does he feel like meeting me? Then I'll see how he answers. You realise he may not answer at all?"

"If he doesn't, we can forget the whole thing." She jumped to her feet. A sheet of paper with Alec's address in Funchal was on top of a heap of papers on the flap of the Georgian bureau, as if she had been very sure of Peter and had had it ready for him. "Now let's look at my drawings, then we'll have lunch. Avocados and cold duck and cheese. I didn't want to waste any of your time here doing a lot of cooking. Come along."

She went swiftly to the door, dodging one or two pieces of furniture and apparently only just missing knocking over a precious old Worcester jug with an elbow. Peter put Alec's address in his pocket and followed her.

The drawings, as he had expected, were excellent. In the story Edward Otter and his friends and followers had arranged a summit meeting with the mink to discuss whether peace between them might be possible in view of a potentially serious menace that had appeared in their disputed territory. This was a singularly large animal that walked on two legs, wore strangely shaped coverings on its feet apparently made of animal skins, and whose intentions towards them were obscure. A kind of helpfulness towards them alternated with shocking ferocity. No more than the boots worn by this animal ever appeared in Clare's drawings, trampling down delightful flowers and ferns. She was particularly gifted when it came to plant drawings. She managed to make their desecration by the great boots truly tragic.

Edward Otter himself had a statesmanlike look of dignity and dependability. The mink looked sly and unreliable. The round table at which they gathered for their discussions was covered with a cloth edged with little bobbles and had a pot filled with buttercups and daisies in the middle of it. Peter praised the drawings warmly. He also praised the lunch at which nothing more was said about Alec, but when he left after it, he still had an uneasy feeling that he was being sent to Madeira by Clare as an ambassador to her husband to find out how he would view her re-entry into his life.

There was a good deal of bitter humour in the situation, but on the whole Peter wished her success. It would settle a number of things for himself, without there having to be anything so unpleasant as a rupture. Just a final break, quietly and peaceably made. Painful at first, but a good thing for them both in the end. The only trouble was that he had not the slightest belief that it would ever come about, because Alec would not even consider it.

Peter did not believe that Alec would answer his letter either, but he wrote to him that evening, saying that he was thinking of taking a holiday on Madeira and would like to see him again, if the thought of this appealed to him too. Then, on his usual two-mile walk, Peter posted the letter and after that put the whole thing out of his mind. He had been thinking, before he had seen Clare, of three weeks in the Highlands, walking, fishing, and looking for a new background for the next adventure of Edward Otter. Would it be possible, he wondered, to use Madeira for this? Were there otters there? Could Edward possibly have chums in the mountain streams whom he might visit?

Not that Peter had ever worried much about realism where his hero was concerned, but he had never tried sending him abroad before and was not sure how it would work out. There was no need to think about this, however, since Alec would not answer.

But he did answer after about a week. He wrote:

Dear Peter,

Good to hear from you after all this time. Yes, if you're coming here, of course we must meet. In fact, unless you've fixed things up in a hotel already, which no doubt would be more luxurious, why don't you stay with me? I've an adequate spare room and you can come and go as you like. I'm fairly occupied, so you could feel quite free and you'd be welcome. But stick to your hotel if you'd sooner, we can meet all the same. I read one of your books recently, out of curiosity. I'm told adults read them as well as children. Anthropomorphism is the thing nowadays, isn't it? Lucky for you to have hit on a market like that.

Hoping to see you, yours,

Alec

"Lucky!" Peter said to himself explosively. "He thinks it's all luck and not just damned, slogging hard work!"

But writing back to Alec, he said that he would be delighted to stay with him, then he telephoned Clare and told her what had happened.

She sounded oddly doubtful, almost as if, since he had seen her, she had changed her mind about wanting him to visit Alec. But still she thanked him, saying that she was sure that in any case he would enjoy a stay on Madeira, even if he and Alec no longer hit it off.

Feeling rather resentfully that perhaps she had never intended him to take her seriously, as she understood perfectly the absurdity of her demands, and that she had been merely indulging a very superficial mood of nostalgia which she had now got over, Peter set off to Cook's in Berkeley Street to book his flight to Funchal.

Then he walked along Piccadilly to Simpson's to buy himself some tropical weight trousers. He also bought some new shirts, more colourful than he usually wore, which helped to give him a holiday feeling, and by the time all his preparations had been made, he had almost forgotten that this was not simply a holiday he was taking, but that he was supposed to be going to Funchal on a mission.

CHAPTER 2

The morning of the day of his departure
was grey and damp, with the sky lost
behind clouds and a sharp little wind
blowing, of the kind that can make May
seem almost wintry. The aeroplane, which
left Heathrow at four-ten, direct for
Funchal, was only half full. Peter settled
down by a window and took a Rex Stout
paperback out of the canvas bag that he
had brought with him. He had packed a
number of paperbacks into his suitcase.
Alec had never gone in much for books
and Peter could easily imagine arriving at
the house, flat, or whatever it was that
Alec lived in and finding that there was
nothing whatever to read.

No one sat down in the seat next to Peter, but a young man took the one beyond it, next to the gangway, and also began to read. Peter read only for a little while, then, as the sign telling passengers to keep their seat belts fastened was switched off and the feeling of climbing ended, he let the book sink on to his knee and sat gazing down at the clouds beneath them.

Far below the whole sky consisted of those clouds, while up here it was an immensity of blue. As always, when he flew, he found it difficult to believe that so much shining brightness could be invisible on the earth. There was a perversity about it, a feeling almost of deliberate wastefulness on the part of whatever powers organised such things. Up here the sun gave no special joy or exhilaration, when down below it could have brought delight. But at least on Madeira, it was to be assumed, he would see plenty of it, as well as a sparkling sea and exotic flowers. He started to read again. But once more he found his attention wandering as he began to wonder what had made Alec Methven settle there.

When Peter had last seen Alec he had just resigned from the Hong Kong police force and had been about to leave for the Congo, as it had still been called then, to fight as a mercenary. Peter had never known for sure if Alec's determination to do this had been the cause or the result of the breakup of his marriage. Clare had appeared oddly indifferent to the matter. She had shrugged her shoulders and said that if that was the sort of thing he wanted to do, he had better get on with it. She had returned to England and so far as Peter knew, had never seen Alec again. But there had been no divorce because, so she had always said, it would be troublesome and not worth her while. If she ever felt like marrying again, which she did not think was likely, she could see about it then.

Meanwhile Alec must at some time have got tired of wandering and settled down, which seemed strange, considering how restless he had always been. Before Hong Kong he had been a pilot for an air-taxi company, and before that in the R.A.F. He had always craved action. But nothing lasted long with him. He had married soon after arriving in Hong Kong, where Clare had been working as a secretary to the manager of one of the larger banks. She had gone on working for some time after her marriage, in fact, until Edward Otter had come into her life and given her another source of income. She had never considered Alec's income as a policeman enough for the two of them to live on.

Peter had met them at one of the endless cocktail parties that made up their social life and had become intimate with them surprisingly quickly. He had still been a newcomer at the university and was lonely and the Methvens had intrigued him from the start. Alec could hardly have been more unlike him and yet had seemed extremely interested in Peter's work and way of living and almost regretful that such things were beyond him. In those days Clare had claimed that Peter liked Alec much better than he liked her and perhaps there had been some truth in this. Anyway, he had not yet fallen in love with her and still found that it was as a couple that he enjoyed their company. And really it would have been very convenient if only that had lasted.

Drinks were being served on the aeroplane. The young man in the same row as Peter ordered a gin and tonic and Peter whisky. As he sipped it he found that the man was looking at him with a certain interest. When their eyes met, he smiled.

"May's the wrong month for Madeira, you know," he said. "The weather may be foul."

He was not more than twenty-five, long and bony, with a shock of wavy, light brown hair, a round, fresh-coloured face and friendly grey eyes. He was wearing jeans, a red and white checked shirt, and a jacket of rather soiled fawn corduroy.

"I've never been there before," Peter answered. "Do you know it well?"

"I've been there a few times." The young man had a very agreeable voice, light and soft and clear and oddly intimate. "I've some family there whom I visit from time to time. You're going to one of the hotels, I expect."

"No, as a matter of fact, I'm going to stay with a friend," Peter said.

"In Funchal?"

"Yes."

"Dreary little place, Funchal," the young man said. "It used to be rather attractive, but in the last few years it's changed a lot, hotels springing up right and left, and there's much too much traffic and an appalling lot of noise. The streets are solid with taxis and everyone keeps his thumb on the horn. Of course you can find quiet if you get out into the mountains."

"Perhaps I'll do that." Peter could not remember if Alec was likely to want to walk in the mountains. In Hong Kong such matters had not arisen. But Peter's feeling was that Alec would in any case be grateful if he kept himself occupied a fair amount on his own. Alec had always been a man who seemed best satisfied with a good deal of his own company.

The young man chattered on, while dinner was served and cleared away, about the other places that he had visited, various Aegean islands, Sardinia, Kenya, Mexico. But because of the way that all the young dress nowadays, it was impossible to guess whether he could afford what must have been costly journeys because he was a success in some kind of job, or was dependent on a wealthy family.

His voice was the only clue to his background and even there it was impossible to guess whether he had acquired it at a public school or at some drama school. It seemed to Peter that there was something theatrical about him. He had the actor's eagerness to please, to project a charming image. Also there were moments when Peter suddenly had the feeling that he had seen him before and wondered if perhaps he actually had, say on television or in the theater.

But then, abruptly, almost without warning, the young man fell asleep. He gave Peter a winning smile, closed his eyes, folded his hands across his stomach, and was asleep in a moment. Peter returned to Rex Stout. It would not be so very long now before they landed. The clouds beneath them were as dense as ever and even when the first sinking feeling came as the aeroplane began to lose height, there was no glitter of the sea to be seen, but only the still, frothy white mass that stretched to the horizon.

When the island suddenly appeared beneath them, it was as if they had forced open a lid and slid in under it, so close to the ground that it was a shock to see it there, almost within hailing distance. Slopes that perhaps were the base of mountains disappeared in low mist, with no peaks to be seen. There was no evening sunshine on the green countryside, or on the red and white villages along the coast, and the Atlantic, beating at the foot of high black cliffs, was a sullen grey. The aeroplane seemed to be flying almost level with the cliffs, then came to rest on a narrow runway carved out between a hillside and a steep drop to the ocean.

The young man, whom a stewardess had had to wake some minutes before to make him fasten his seat belt, yawned and stretched and said that he had enjoyed travelling with Peter. Then Peter lost sight of him in the crowd that surged through the very casual customs and out into the open where friends and relatives and hotel touts and taxi drivers were waiting to meet them.

In spite of the clouds covering the sky the air felt very warm after the cold wind of May in London. It was a slight disappointment to Peter that Alec was not there, but when he came to think of it, he was not even sure if Alec possessed a car. How poor was he after that adventure of his in the Congo? It was unlikely that he had emerged from it with much more than the clothes that he wore. However, he had emerged at least with his life, which could be regarded as considerable good fortune. Peter was prepared to find him living in squalor. Clean and tidy squalor, because that was what Alec was like, but it seemed unlikely that he would be able to offer Peter much in the way of comforts.

He found a long line of taxis waiting at the airport. Taking one, thankful that the driver spoke a certain amount of English and wondering if perhaps he was one of Alec's pupils, he gave him Alec's address, then settled back, realising all at once that he had no intention of probing into Alec's affairs or doing anything that Clare had asked him. This was simply to be a meeting between two people who had once been good friends and who might be able to pick up the threads that would renew that old pleasant relationship. If they could not, if they had drifted too hopelessly apart, Peter would move to a hotel.

The drive into Funchal was longer than he had expected. The traffic on the sharply bending road was hair-raising and the taxi driver lightheartedly confident at each blind corner that he had the right of way. They passed through several villages of small, cream-coloured houses with roofs of red pantiles and with enormous slogans crudely painted on their walls. Political slogans, Peter presumed, though they were incomprehensible to him, and he felt that the great black and red letters expressed an irresponsible kind of ferocity which gave the quiet villages a look of feverish aggression, a kind of menace.

But in the gardens there were glowing bushes of hibiscus, clumps of agapanthus, and lovely pale blue clusters of plumbago that looked silver in the dusk. The dusk was coming rapidly. It had been daylight when the taxi left the airport, but by the time that it swooped, horn blaring, into the dense traffic of Funchal, it was twilight.

They drove along what Peter took to be the main street of the town before curving off to the right, up a steep hill. A minute or two later the taxi stopped. It was in a quiet street of medium-sized houses that had a comfortable, middle-class air about them. Most of them had high walls round their gardens, pierced by wrought-iron gates. Peter fumbled clumsily with a bundle of escudos that he had obtained before leaving London, taking some time to count out the amount of his fare and to add a tip which he hoped was appropriate. Then he picked up his suitcase and his canvas bag, turned to the gate that had Alec's number on it, and pushed it open.

The house beyond it was small, of one storey only, with a roof of wide, upward curving eaves that gave it a faintly oriental appearance. Bougainvillea that looked almost black in the near-darkness, hung in thick curtains on either side of the door. Peter went up to it and pressed the bell beside it.

He heard it ringing inside the house, but there was no reply to it. Nor were there any lights on in the house. He rang again, waited and rang a third time. Irritated, thinking that it was one thing for Alec not to have come to the airport to meet him, but quite another not to be at home to receive him, Peter grasped his luggage and set off prowling round the house to see if there was any other entrance.

He might, he thought, find Alec in the garden, for on a mild, still evening like this it would have been pleasant to sit out of doors to wait for his guest, then not impossible to fall asleep. Going down some steps at the side of the house, Peter reached the corner of it, saw a sloping lawn, the shapes of palm trees against the evening sky, and shadowy, tattered masses of bananas.

Then he saw Alec.

He was lying stretched out in a cane chair on a small patio and sound asleep.

So soundly asleep, Peter saw at a glance, that there would never be any waking him. Close to his chair on the paving stones of the patio lay a small gun. There was a dark hole on one side of his head and blood thickened around it.

Peter went rigid, then stooped quickly and touched one of Alec's cheeks. It had a chill that jabbed his nerves like the blade of a knife. He was very ignorant of such things, but it seemed to him that to be so cold Alec must have been dead for many hours.

CHAPTER 3

Later it was to bewilder Peter how little surprise he felt at that moment. Shock, yes, but it was as if he had always known that sooner or later Alec would do this, that a will to self-destruction had always been there and that there was nothing astonishing about the fact that he had committed suicide.

At the time Peter did not question that this was suicide. It did not even cross his mind that it might be murder. That came later. Nevertheless, he realised at once that the first thing that he must do was to call the police. The need for a doctor was long past. The police would bring one, for their own purposes, but Alec had been beyond help from the instant that that hole had been drilled into his head.

Backing a few steps away from his long, still body, which was clothed in crumpled cotton trousers and a dark blue shirt, Peter thought how little his face had changed in fifteen years, though perhaps it was death that had erased the lines that should have been and left the look of calm that had never been there in his lifetime. He had been a good-looking man, with a long, narrow face and strong, sharply defined features. He had been well built too, though given to little starts and fidgets, as if he had found it almost impossible to relax. At times, when he had been upset for some reason, he had stuttered slightly. A man, Peter had always thought, who had been driven on by some incessant tension inside him.

But his life here could hardly have been one of action. Perhaps he had found peace of a kind before his death. Peter turned away towards the house. Glass doors stood open, leading into what he could just see in the near-darkness was a living room. Dimly he saw the shapes of chairs and walls lined with books and some shadowy pictures. It took him a moment to find a light switch. Then, as light filled the room, he saw what he was looking for, a telephone, and he had his hand on it before he realised that he had not the slightest idea how to call the police on this island and that in any case it would probably have to be done in Portuguese.

His hand dropped to his side. He became aware of the fact that in spite of the warmth of the evening, he felt extremely cold. Also, although his hand was quite steady, he felt as if inwardly he was shaking helplessly. Shock, of course, and a drink would help if he could find where Alec kept it. But somehow he had to get in touch with the police. He looked warily at the telephone, as if it might play some unpleasant trick on him, and was wondering how it would respond if he tried English on it when a bell rang shrilly in the silent house.

He started violently, thinking for a moment that it was the telephone beside him ringing; then he realised that it had been the front door bell. That might mean help, a visitor who understood the local telephones, who could speak the language. He went to the door of the room, finding himself in a small hall which the light from behind him showed him had several doors opening out of it, all of them closed. Finding a light switch, he turned it on, then opened the front door.

The young man with whom he had chatted on the aeroplane stood outside it. He looked very surprised at seeing Peter.

"Hallo," he said. "Is my uncle the friend you were coming to visit here?"

"Your uncle?" Peter said. "I didn't know he'd any relations."

"Yes, my mother was his sister. Dead long ago. I suppose we're each other's only relatives now. Isn't he around?"

"Yes . . . That is . . . Well . . ." Feeling the helplessness that had afflicted him ever since he had come into the house, Peter paused, looking stupidly at the young man.

He said, "D'you mind if I come in, then?"

Peter realised that he had been blocking

the doorway. He moved hastily to one side.

The young man stepped into the house, bringing his suitcase with him, and closed the door behind him. He had turned towards the door of the living room when Peter checked him with a hand on his arm.

"Just a moment," he said. "I'd better warn you, there's been an accident — no, damn it, why should I say that? There was nothing accidental about it, but I don't know the right way to break bad news. The fact is, Alec's dead. He's out on the patio and it's obvious he's shot himself."

He saw a flicker of disbelief on the young man's face, then blankness and a sudden pallor. Shaking off Peter's hand, he strode into the living room and across it to the glass doors that opened on to the patio. Following him, Peter realised why he had had the feeling that he had seen the young man before. In spite of the fact that there was almost no similarity in their features, his face had an odd likeness to Alec's. The stranger's face was round, Alec's was long. Alec's features were hard and firmly modelled, his nephew's rather soft and indeterminate. His hair was light brown, Alec's much darker. Yet perhaps in the eyes or in something about the lips and the way they moved, there was that elusive thing, a family likeness.

Peter waited in the doorway till the young man, who had stood still close to Alec, looking down at him in silence, turned slowly and looked at him.

"Who are you, anyway?" he asked. His voice was as pleasant as ever, but he spoke abruptly.

"My name's Peter Corey," Peter answered. "I used to know Alec in Hong Kong."

He was thankful that the name seemed to mean nothing special to the young man.

"My name's Michael Searle," he said. "What do we do now?"

"We call the police," Peter said. "Can you speak Portuguese?"

"Not a word."

"Then we'll have to see how it works in English."

"But I can't understand it!" Michael Searle exploded. "He asked me specially to come, said it was too long since we'd seen each other last, and then . . . D'you think there could have been some reason for his wanting to arrange this? D'you know anything about why he should have done it?''

''I haven't seen him for fifteen years,'' Peter said. ''I don't know anything about his recent life.''

''He'd everything he wanted, so he always wrote. Said he'd had luck, great luck, and had the sense to stick to the life that suited him. D'you think that was all untrue?''

''How can we tell? For all we know, he'd recently discovered some incurable illness, or something like that.''

''But to do this just when he'd specially asked me to come to see him!''

''Me too,'' Peter said.

Michael Searle looked mildly surprised at being reminded that Peter was involved in the situation.

''Yes, of course, you too.''

''D'you know how long he's lived on Madeira?'' Peter asked.

''About seven years.''

"And always been so content?"

"I don't know about that. I was only eighteen or thereabouts when he settled here. If he'd had troubles I don't suppose he'd have told me about them. They weren't financial. He used to give me money when I was at Cambridge to help out the grant I had, which wouldn't have gone far without him. He was always wonderfully generous. . . ." There was a tremor in his voice. "He was mad on education too, said it was what he'd missed out on all his life. He wanted me to be a scientist or a scholar or something like that. It was pretty much of a disappointment for him when it turned out I simply hadn't got it in me."

"Well, we'd better try to cope with this telephone," Peter said, and picked it up. "I wonder how one dials Operator."

"No, wait a moment." Searle's hand shot out, took the telephone away from Peter and put it back on its stand. "I know what we'll do. There are some English people living opposite, friends of Alec's who've been here for years and I'm sure speak Portuguese. If you'll go across

43

and tell them what's happened, they'll do the telephoning for us. Their name's Raven. I think the number of the house is 17. I can't remember for sure, but it's the house facing this, a sort of pale blue house with little wrought-iron balconies. They were very good friends of Alec's. I know they'll help.''

Peter felt inclined to suggest that since Michael Searle knew the Ravens, it would be better for him to go over to see them himself, than for Peter, a stranger. But he thought it was possible that the young man, who had managed to maintain a stiff, artificial sort of calm, was nearer to breaking down than it appeared and needed some time to himself, perhaps to shed tears, perhaps only to come close for the last time to the man who had loved and helped him.

''All right, I'll see what I can do,'' Peter said, and turned back into the living room to go to the front door and out into the street.

But in the middle of the room he paused and looked round him.

It was not at all the kind of room that

he would have expected Alec Methven to create around himself to give him the contentment he had claimed to have found. The walls were covered with books almost to the ceiling, some of them fine editions. There was a hi-fi and a long rack filled with records. There were some watercolour seascapes wherever the bookcases left room for them, not outstanding but attractive. There were some fine Persian rugs on the tiled floor. The chairs looked deep and comfortable. It was altogether a very comfortable room, almost luxurious, for someone who liked reading and music, but not for the Alec whom Peter had known fifteen years before.

But people can change. And certainly Clare's fear that Alec might be living in poverty had no foundation.

Peter let himself out into the garden and crossed the street. The night had become very dark. No moonlight or starlight penetrated the low clouds. There were lamps along the street, but in their light the houses on the other side all looked merely pale. If one of them was light blue, the colour did not show. But one just opposite Alec's, a two-storey house, had 17 on the pillar beside the gate and had small wrought-iron balconies at its upper windows. Peter pushed open the gate, went to the door, and rang the bell.

It was answered at once by quick footsteps and the door was opened. A young girl stood there, looking at Peter with wide, startled brown eyes. It was as if she found a visitor at that hour very surprising, or else had been expecting someone else and it was the sight of a stranger that was astonishing.

She looked about eighteen, a slim girl in a long, loose, flowered cotton dress and sandals with very high heels, so that she seemed almost as tall as Peter. Her hair was dark, long and straight, spread out over her shoulders. She was not a very pretty girl, though it looked as if she had tried to be one. She wore shiny pink lipstick and a great deal of make-up round her eyes. But her face, in spite of its tan, was pale, thin, and nervous. Staring at Peter, she put a hand to her mouth, as if to stop herself from saying something. It was a very childish gesture.

"Miss Raven?" he said.

"No, I'm Sarah Baird," she said, speaking round her hand. "If you want my godmother, she's in the garden. I'll get her, shall I? But she's Mrs. Raven, not Miss."

"I'm sorry. Yes, can I see her — or Mr. Raven?"

She let her hand drop to her side. "It's Colonel Raven, and don't forget that. You'll find it's important."

"I see. Thanks. I'm sorry to disturb them, but it's something very urgent. I'm a friend of Alec Methven's and I'm told they're friends of his too, and he — I mean, I need help."

"Why? Is something the matter? Has something happened to him?"

With so much mascara round her eyes it was difficult to interpret their expression, but he had an impression that although he had not yet told her anything, she looked frightened.

"I'm afraid so, yes," he said. "But can I see Colonel or Mrs. Raven?"

Her hand went to her mouth again.

"Who are you?"

"My name's Corey."

"Oh, my goodness, you're the man who writes!" she exclaimed. "Alec lent me one of your books once. He said he used to know you. Come in. I'll get Harriet."

She turned and went running across the hall into one of the rooms opening out of it, leaving Peter to follow her.

It was a stiff, dull room. Only a picture briefly caught Peter's eye, a seascape that looked very like the ones that hung in Alec's room. It showed high black cliffs, like those that he had seen from the aeroplane, with white foam frothing over the rocks at their base. But then a woman came into the room through glass doors that led out on to a lighted patio very like Alec's and he turned away from the picture to meet her.

She was about forty, tall, slender, with large dark eyes and silver-grey hair swept up from a face that was still unlined, although it had an expression of anxiety which it seemed to Peter must be printed on it and not been brought there simply by whatever the girl had told her. She was wearing a kind of kaftan made of turquoise-coloured silk and walked with a slightly stooping, hesitant kind of grace.

"I'm Mrs. Raven," she said. "Sarah tells me you're Mr. Corey, Alec's friend, and that something's happened to him."

"Yes, it's very bad news, I'm afraid," Peter said. "It seems he's shot himself."

"Shot himself — he's dead?" The woman's voice went up sharply with a horrified gasp.

"Yes, I arrived by plane this evening — I got to the house just a little while ago — and I found him. . . ." Peter was wishing that he had sent Michael Searle over to break the news. "I found him in a chair on the patio, with a gun on the ground beside him. I don't know anything about such things, but I think he must have been dead for several hours."

"How terrible, how — how unbelievable!" The woman's face had grown haggard all in a moment and her big eyes filled with fear. Had they all got frightened eyes in this house, Peter wondered. "But you want our help. What can we do?"

"We ought to telephone for the police," Peter said, "but I can't speak the language and don't know how to set about it. I was wondering if you'd do it for me."

"Yes, of course. At once. But how terrible for you to have come here and found him — like that. Dead? You're absolutely sure he's dead? We oughtn't to get a doctor first?"

"I'm afraid there isn't any doubt of it."

Behind her the girl suddenly cried out, "It can't be, it can't be! I don't believe it!"

Abruptly she left the room and Peter heard her running up the stairs, chattering wildly to herself.

As if she felt that she had to apologise for this, Mrs. Raven said, "I'm sorry, Mr. Corey. She's very devoted to Alec. She really loves him. He's been so good to her. I think I ought to go to her. She hasn't been very well lately."

"The telephone," Peter said.

"Yes, yes, of course. But I'll get my husband to do it. That'll be best. James —" She went to the patio doors and looked out. "James, please come in. A dreadful thing's happened. Alec's shot himself and Mr. Corey, who only got to Madeira this evening, found him and wants us to telephone the police for him."

CHAPTER 4

There was a sliding sound on the ground outside, as if a chair were being pushed back, then there was silence. Peter wondered if it was possible that the man outside had no intention of coming in to help. But then he discovered the reason for the pause. The man who appeared in the doorway moved very slowly, leaning on a stick. He was at least twenty years older than his wife, very tall and gaunt, with thick white hair, narrow blue eyes, and the bitter, strained face of someone who lived in constant pain. He was wearing a well-tailored fawn suit, a white shirt, and a dark brown tie.

He held out a hand to Peter. In spite of

the warmth of the evening, it was cold and dry.

"Did I get that right?" he asked. His voice had a disagreeable rasp in it. "Alec's committed suicide? That doesn't make sense. I had a drink with him only yesterday evening. Everything was perfectly normal. He told me you were coming and seemed to be looking forward to it and he said something about that nephew of his. He always cared more about him than the young fellow deserved, that's my opinion. Anyway, he's hardly ever come here to visit his uncle. But what is it you want me to do? Phone the police?"

"Please," Peter said, trying to control his impatience.

"I'm going upstairs to Sarah," Mrs. Raven said. "You'll forgive me, won't you, Mr. Corey? It's just that I think this is a terrible shock for her and I don't like to think of leaving her alone. I'll come down again in a moment."

She flitted out of the room, the folds of her silk dress billowing out behind her.

"Come along," Colonel Raven said to

Peter. "The telephone's in the other room." He limped towards the door, leaning heavily on his stick. "Sorry I'm so slow. Bloody arthritis. Got wounded in the knee in Burma, that's what's supposd to have started it up, then later I had two operations, but they didn't seem to help, so in the end we came out here with the idea that the climate might do something for me. All very well, but with the pound going down and down life's getting too damned expensive. By the way, don't worry about that crazy girl. My wife's devoted to her, but she just wants attention, she isn't really too terribly upset. She'll be perfectly all right by tomorrow. The police now. Ah yes. Poor old Alec. I had a drink with him only yesterday — but I told you that, didn't I? I hope he made a clean job of it, didn't suffer."

"Very clean," Peter said.

"That's good, that's good. Well now, here we are." He had lowered himself cautiously on to a chair beside the telephone in another dull little room, which appeared to be the dining room.

"Just give me a moment while I find out how to call the police. We've never had much truck with them here, only registering as resident aliens and so on."

He picked up the telephone, dialled, and spoke into it in fluent Portuguese.

As he put it down again, he said, "They'll be out right away. You'll want to get back to the other house, I expect. Shall I come with you?"

"It might be a great help," Peter said. "There's the language problem, for one thing."

"Oh, you won't find any difficulty there," the colonel said. "They'll all speak English. This island's existed on the tourist trade for a long time, ever since the days when the wealthy British took to coming out here for their tuberculosis. All that's stopped, of course. The sanatoria have closed down. But English is almost a second language. I'll come all the same. I may be of some use."

He got slowly to his feet, grasping his stick again.

As he limped out into the hall his wife came hurrying down the stairs.

"She's locked herself in and told me to go away," she said. "I don't know what to do."

"Leave her for once to handle things in her own way," he answered. "Don't fuss so much about her."

"I'm not fussing," she said. "It's just that . . ." She turned to Peter, making a fluttery gesture with her hands. "I suppose I *am* fussing, but it's just that she isn't well. She had a nervous breakdown about a year ago, before she came out to stay with us. Her father died suddenly of a heart attack and that left her quite alone. Her mother died of cancer when she was only three, you see, so she's never had anyone but him and they were absolutely devoted to one another. When I went over to London to see if I could help I found her in a terrible state, so I brought her back with me and she's been recovering by degrees. I've been feeling very hopeful about her lately. But I don't know what Alec's death will do to her. He's the only person who's seemed to mean anything to her, I think because in some way he reminds her of her father. I think she may easily have a bad relapse."

"D'you know, you're talking as if she and her relapses are a lot more important than Alec and what's happened to him?" her husband said. "For God's sake, don't worry so much about the wretched child. She's found a comfortable berth here and she doesn't mean to leave it. A job is what she needs, but she's bone idle. And what's she put all that muck on her face for today? She hasn't done that before."

"Oh, I thought it was a good sign," the woman said. "Of course she overdid it, but it's almost the first sign she's given of caring how she looks to other people. If she wants to go on with it, I'll teach her a little about how to do it."

"Well, if you don't mind," Peter said, feeling that this argument about the girl could go on indefinitely, "I'll be getting back. Searle — Alec's nephew — is there on his own. I'll tell him the police are coming."

"Yes, yes," Colonel Raven said. "I'm sorry this talk has been holding us up. Let's go. Coming, Harriet?"

She hesitated with a glance at the stairs,

then said, "Yes, I'll come."

"No need for it," he said. "Nothing you can do. You can stay with the girl, if you'd sooner."

"She doesn't want me for the present, but I won't leave her for long." She opened the front door and walked out into the night, a slender, elegant presence going ahead of the two men to the house across the road.

Peter would have been just as pleased if she had decided to stay at home. She seemed to him too nervous and timorous to be of much use. Yet the strange thing was that when she saw the long, still form of Alec Methven in the chair on the patio, she became very calm. It was as if she and death were well acquainted and she found nothing fearsome in the sight of it. She stood looking down at Alec with a detached kind of pity. Then she looked up at Peter, who was still far more shaken than she appeared to be, and said, "I think you need a drink."

Colonel Raven, who had followed her slowly out to the patio, remarked, "My wife used to be a nurse. We can all do with a drink, if you can find the doings.''

They had been let into the house by Michael Searle, who was standing now in the middle of the living room, looking helpless.

He said, ''I'll go and look for them. I expect they're in the dining room.''

But as he turned to leave the room, Mrs. Raven, coming in from the patio, said, ''Michael! It's a long time since you were here last — two years at least, isn't it? I know Alec was very much looking forward to your coming. Did you get here just this evening?''

Peter decided that if she wanted to converse with Searle, he would leave her to it and went looking for the drinks himself.

He did not know which of the doors that opened out of the hall led into the dining room, so he tried the nearest. It turned out that it led into what was obviously Alec's bedroom, a room with white walls and built-in furniture, all white, with the exception of a fine old mahogany tallboy that stood between two windows.

Peter stood staring at it. All its drawers were open and clothes had been tumbled out of them on to the floor. The doors of the painted white wardrobe were open and the suits hanging inside it had been roughly pushed to one end. Shoes had been scattered on the floor. A picture on one wall hung crooked, as if someone had been looking behind it. Someone had made a hasty search here and had either been interrupted or had not cared who discovered it.

But when had it been done?

It was then, standing there, looking at the chaos, that Peter asked himself for the first time if Alec's death had really been suicide.

But the question only flickered through his mind and faded. The thought of murder was still too bizarre for him to consider it seriously. It would turn out, he thought, that there was some quite simple explanation for this search, the most likely being that Alec himself was responsible. Perhaps in the last moments before he killed himself he had felt some desperate need to find something, something that he had wanted to destroy, or to give to someone, or to leave as an explanation of his action.

But for the moment there was nothing to be done about it. The police would want everything left as it was. Peter closed the door softly, discovered that the one next to it led into the dining room, found bottles and glasses on a tray on the sideboard, and carried the tray through to the room where Searle and the Ravens were waiting. He poured out drinks for them all, but for some reason not quite clear to himself, said nothing about what he had found in Alec's bedroom.

However, as he moved restlessly about the room while the others sat down, he began to wish that he had taken the opportunity, while he was out of the room, of looking in the other rooms in Alec's small house to see if they had suffered the same kind of searching as his bedroom. But to go out now to do this would be conspicuous.

He was still thinking of this when Mrs. Raven exclaimed, "But why? *Why?*" She swallowed most of her whisky at a gulp.

Her large dark eyes burned in her pale face. She had lost her look of calm and appeared tense and anxious again. "Loneliness, was that it? He was a very lonely man, I always thought. He hadn't any friends. We were about as close to him as anyone, but we weren't really friends, we were just acquaintances, neighbours. Would a person kill himself out of loneliness, d'you think?"

The question seemed to be addressed to no one in particular and nobody answered it. But after a moment Peter said, "He *was* lonely, I suppose?"

"I didn't think so," Colonel Raven said. "It isn't everyone who needs other people all the time. Most of us waste too much of our time on all that social nonsense we get involved in. I thought he seemed a pretty sensible sort of chap who'd found a way of living that suited him and he was a lot more contented than most of us."

"That isn't what I meant exactly," Peter said. "I've been wondering since I came into this house if there was anyone in his life who had a good deal of influence over him. A woman, perhaps. Someone, anyway, who'd formed his tastes in recent years. The Alec I used to know hadn't much time for books or music or painting.''

"They're his own paintings, did you know that?" Harriet Raven said. "I always thought that if only he'd got started earlier he might have developed into something quite outstanding. But he was very modest about them. He said he just did them for his own pleasure and didn't care what anyone else thought of them.''

"You haven't answered his question," Colonel Raven said with a sudden roughness in his harsh voice. "Was there a woman in his life?''

"No, there wasn't," she said quickly.

She twisted her long, thin fingers together, looking up at Peter with what seemed almost an air of defiance, as if he might challenge her. It occurred to him that, allowing for her curious look of uncertainty about herself, she was an uncommonly beautiful woman. But for a nurse she seemed remarkably fragile.

Nursing is not a profession that has much use for tender plants. She must be much stronger than she appeared, he thought.

"I wonder how you can be so sure of that," her husband said with the same roughness. "Did he tell you everything about himself?"

"For Christ's sake!" Michael Searle exploded suddenly. "The way you're talking! He's lying out there dead and you're talking — talking as if — oh, good God, it isn't decent! A woman in his life! If there was one, it was his own business, wasn't it?"

"But if we knew it might help us to understand what's happened, mightn't it?" Peter said quietly.

"And that was his own business too!" the young man said violently. "He wanted to die and that was that. What right has any of us got to pry into his reasons?"

In theory Peter agreed with him. If the time should ever come when he wanted to take his own life, he would feel, he was sure, that his reasons for doing it were entirely private and that any message that he would leave behind would be entirely false. It would just be some meaningless platitude, designed to make things easier for other people. But the thought of that ravished bedroom of Alec's remained in his mind, making him feel that there was something mysterious and important that must be discovered about Alec.

Pouring out some more whisky for himself, he said, "The police will pry into it, I expect, if they're normally efficient. That can't be helped."

"Well, I can tell you, there wasn't any woman," Searle said. "His marriage was such a failure that he never wanted to get entangled again."

"Isn't it two years since you saw him last?" Peter said. "A lot can happen in two years."

"Not in these last two," Harriet Raven said. She came to her feet out of the deep chair in which she had been half reclining. "The painting and the books and the music go back to the time when we knew him first. Of course, he added to them all since then, but it wasn't because of anyone's influence. I sometimes thought, when he came here, that for the first time in his life he must have got the time and the money to develop the things in which he was really interested. Now I'm going back to Sarah. Do you remember Sarah, Michael? You met her here, didn't you, when she was a child? I'll tell her you're here. She isn't — she isn't very well, but I'm sure she'll want to see you."

"Harriet means the girl's bonkers," the colonel growled. "Sheer egotism, most of it. No self-control, no consideration for other people. Nervous breakdown — bah! If that was so, she ought to be in a home."

Harriet gave a sad little shake of her head. "He doesn't really mean it," she said to Searle, who had got quickly to his feet when she did. "He's very fond of her."

"I know she's been living on us for a year when she's rich enough to buy us out," her husband said. "Anyway, we shan't stay here much longer, with the pound going down and down, then she'll have to get back to England and stand on her own two feet, and damn good for her too, that's my opinion."

"You know it isn't really," his wife said gently. "You want to help her as much as I do. Well, if the police want me, I'll be at home and I can come back here or they can see me there, whichever they choose. Not that there's any help I can give them." She put a hand on Searle's arm. "I'm so sorry about this, Michael, terribly sorry. If there's anything at all we can do, come and tell us. We were very fond of Alec, you know. I thought he was a very rare sort of person. Something special."

"Yes, he was all right," the colonel muttered.

She turned to Peter. "Mr. Corey, you too — if there's anything we can do, let us know. I expect you'll be staying on at least for a little while, won't you?"

Peter had not the slightest wish to stay on. He would have liked to catch a plane that evening, if there was one, and return to London. But he knew that it was out of the question. Apart from anything that the police might want of him, there were what are called arrangements to be considered, the funeral among them. He might even have to organize that himself and of course would have to be present at it. And Clare, he thought with a start, would have to be told what had happened. Why had he not thought of that until this moment?

"Yes, I'll be staying on for a time," he said.

"Where will you be staying?"

"Some hotel, I suppose. I was going to stay here, but that's hardly possible now."

"And you, Michael?" she asked.

"Some hotel," he echoed Peter.

"You'll let us know where you are, won't you? And you'll come and see Sarah?" She turned and took one more look at the patio, then she went to the door.

Peter heard the front door open and close as she let herself out of the house. Something that had been said in the last few minutes was haunting him, something that Harriet Raven had said. For a moment it eluded him, then he remembered it. It was her remark that when Alec had come here he had had for the first time in his life the time and the money to develop his real interests. The money, that was the important thing.

There must have been a good deal of it merely to fill those bookshelves, and the hi-fi was an expensive one and all the furniture in the house was good. But where had the money come from? Alec had been a poor man when he left for the Congo. So the question was, what had happened to him since then?

Peter was still pondering this when the doorbell rang and Michael Searle went to open the door. The man who came in was shortish, slender, very good-looking, with dark hair, faintly streaked with grey, big, melancholy eyes and a thin, fine-boned face. Peter was to come to know him as the chefe da policia judiciaria, Raposo.

CHAPTER 5

The *chefe* wore a light blue suit and a snowy shirt. He was accompanied by an *agente da policia,* a thickset man in a grey cotton uniform, with a truncheon hanging from his broad leather belt. That anyone as senior as the chefe had been sent to investigate a straightforward suicide at first struck Peter as strange and it was only later that he realised that the death of a foreigner in Funchal, and that by shooting, was treated automatically as a serious matter.

Colonel Raven limped forward to meet him, speaking at first in Portuguese, but then switching to English as he introduced Peter and Michael Searle. The chefe nodded to each of them, then, followed by the agente, went out to the patio, where they stayed for some minutes, exchanging quiet remarks with one another.

Coming back into the living room, the chefe said in excellent English, with only a faint trace of accent, "This is very sad. I was slightly acquainted with Mr. Methven. We played golf together a few times. But I knew very little about him. We were not at all intimate." He looked at Peter. "Colonel Raven tells me you discovered the body."

"Yes," Peter answered. "I arrived here this evening on the plane that gets in about seven-thirty. I was to have stayed with Mr. Methven for a short time. We were old friends. I was a little surprised that he wasn't at the airport to meet me, but I came straight here by taxi and found him like this."

"He was expecting you, then," the chefe said. "He knew you were coming."

"Oh yes."

Raposo turned to Michael Searle. "And you also arrived this evening?"

"Yes, I came out on the same plane as

Mr. Corey," Searle said. "I was also surprised that my uncle wasn't at the airport and I also took a taxi. I got here, I think, a few minutes after Mr. Corey."

"And Mr. Methven also expected you?"

"Yes, he actually wrote to me a little while ago and asked me to come to see him, as I hadn't been here for so long — about two years. He knew what plane I was getting in on."

"And there was no suicide letter here, nothing addressed to any of you?"

They all shook their heads.

The chefe turned to the telephone, paused for a moment as if he was not sure what he wanted to do, then picked it up and spoke into it for a minute or two.

Putting it down, he said, "An ambulance will soon be here and men to take photographs and such things. Colonel Raven, it would oblige me if you would return to your house with these two gentlemen and wait there till I come. There will be questions I must ask."

"Of course," the colonel said. "We'll all be glad to help in any way we can. Not that I can tell you anything. The thing's a great shock to me. I was having a drink with Methven only yesterday evening. . . . Yes, well, I'll tell you all that later, when you come over. There'll have to be a post-mortem, I suppose."

"Yes, that will be necessary, though there can be little doubt it was a shot from that gun that killed him," Raposo answered. "And it looks as if he pulled the trigger himself, but there is always the possibility that he did not. Certain things about the situation strike me as strange."

"Strange?" Colonel Raven said. "D'you mean to say it could possibly be murder?"

"I would only say it is not impossible," the chefe replied. "For one thing, it is certainly strange that Mr. Methven should have chosen today, when he was expecting his two friends to arrive, to kill himself. Also it is strange, since he knew they were coming, that he left no letter for either of them, particularly as he seems to have been very deliberate about the manner in which he set about committing suicide, reclining comfortably in that chair, arranging matters so tidily. When a man kills himself so quietly, it is usual for him to leave a letter, explaining his action to others. Of course, not all suicides are capable of this. They can be so full of fear and desperation that they are not able to think of what their death can mean to the people who must deal with it. But there are no signs of fear or desperation about Mr. Methven. He died, I think we may say, very calmly."

"I don't think he was a man who knew much about fear," Peter said.

The chefe turned to him. "You knew him well?"

"I used to once, but we hadn't met for fifteen years."

"We will talk then, later. I will follow you presently to Colonel Raven's house."

They accepted that as dismissal and the colonel, Searle, and Peter went out once more into the darkness and crossed the street to the house opposite.

When the colonel opened the door a smell of coffee greeted them. Mrs. Raven and Sarah Baird were sitting side by side on a sofa in the living room; on a low table in front of them was a tray with coffee and cups. The girl had washed her face since Peter had seen her last and the makeup was all gone, but there were no signs that there had been tears in her eyes. She looked fearfully at the three men as they came in, as if she dreaded what they might have to say, her gaze dwelling for an instant longer on Michael Searle than on either of the others, but then she looked down into her cup of coffee without any further show of interest.

"Sarah!" Michael Searle exclaimed.

"Sarah, you do remember Michael, don't you?" Mrs. Raven said, putting a hand on the girl's arm. "You met him when you were here last. You were such friends."

"Were we?" Sarah said in a low voice. "I suppose we were."

"Of course you were," Mrs. Raven said. "Don't you remember how he used to take you walking in the mountains?"

"Oh yes, I remember that, but I shouldn't have said we were really friends," Sarah said in the same toneless voice. "How could we be? I was just a kid."

"I thought we were friends," Searle said. "But I expect it seems much longer ago to you than it does to me."

"Perhaps it does," she said. "It seems years and years ago to me. So much has happened since then."

"Sarah lost her father, did you know that?" Mrs. Raven said to Searle.

"Did she?" he said. "I'm very sorry."

"And now this terrible thing about Alec," Mrs. Raven went on. "It's brought it all back, you see."

"For God's sake!" her husband broke in. "Can't we ever talk about anything but what's going on in Sarah's mind, if it's a fact that she's got one? That policeman over there is talking about the possibility that Alec was murdered. What d'you think about that?"

Harriet Raven's glance went swiftly to his face, then more thoughtfully to Peter's, then to Searle's. Then in a surprisingly calm voice she said, "I'm not sure I wasn't expecting that. Somehow it makes more sense than suicide. Alec was much too strong a person to kill himself. They'll be over here presently, I suppose, to find out if we know anything. Now you'll all have some coffee, won't you? Black, Mr. Corey?"

"Please," Peter said.

"And you, Michael?" she asked as she handed Peter his cup.

"Yes, please, black."

She handed a cup to Searle, then one to her husband. The three of them sat down, Peter thinking, as he chose a chair near the window, how utterly inappropriate she looked in the characterless room. In spite of the air of anxiety that clung to her, there was a vividness about her that demanded a quite different background. He would have enjoyed seeing her surrounded by beautiful things, some of the kind, for instance, that Clare might have spared from her superabundance.

The brown three-piece suite with its velvet cushions, the imitation oriental rugs on the floor, the glass-fronted bookcase filled with sets of books that looked as if they had never been read, the stained oak bureau, all belonged to a world into which it seemed she must have strayed accidentally. But if that was what had happened, if this was her husband's taste and not her own, which after all it well might be, then at least she had accepted it when she accepted him without any effort to assert herself. Peter could easily see that happening. He could not see her willingly taking on a struggle to oppose a will that was not in the habit of having its rightness questioned. Only in her nervous defence of her goddaughter had she shown a degree of strength which hinted at what she might be when her deeper feelings were affected.

Michael Searle was watching the girl with concentration, as if something about her puzzled him. Had she changed very much, Peter wondered, from the young girl whom he had once taken walking in the mountains?

The girl was ignoring Searle. She was sitting very still, except for occasionally raising her cup to her lips, but nevertheless she had succeeded in making herself the centre of the room. The irritation she caused the colonel and Harriet Raven's protectiveness towards her and Searle's deep interest in her made her the most important person there. Even he himself, Peter realised, contributed to this, because he was so intrigued by the effect that she had on the others. She was silent, she was almost motionless, she was not very pretty and probably not very intelligent, yet she managed to command attention by the sheer power of an intense egotism, though without seeming to make any effort to do anything of the kind.

It was about half an hour before the chefe came to the house from across the street. As before, the agente in the grey cotton uniform was with him. There were several cars in the street and an ambulance and a number of men going in and out of the house. Mrs. Raven opened the door to the two policemen and brought them into the living room. Raposo bowed slightly to the people in it and said in a tone of faint apology that it would be a great help if he might put a few questions to them. But then it became clear that he wished to question them separately and that there was something rather more official about his presence than he hoped would be necessary for him to assert.

No one thought of challenging him. Only Sarah put down her cup so abruptly that some coffee slopped into the saucer and, as the colonel hobbled out of the room to talk privately to the chefe in the dining room, said in a whisper to Harriet Raven, "I can't talk to him — I can't! You aren't going to let him make me, are you?"

Harriet gave a helpless little shrug of her shoulders. "You mustn't worry so, dear. He'll only ask you a few things like when you saw Alec last and did he seem depressed and things like that. You want to help him, don't you?"

Sarah said nothing, as if she was not at all sure that she did. Harriet gave a sigh and, looking round, offered Peter and Searle more coffee.

"Such a strange day," she murmured when they brought their cups to be refilled. "I've felt depressed all day. I suppose it doesn't mean anything. I don't believe in premonitions. I thought it was just the weather, the clouds, even a little rain in the afternoon, but warm and sultry, really quite typical for the time of year. But now . . . No, it's just hindsight to say I felt there was something wrong. There've been so many things wrong lately. Don't take any notice of me. I'm not often like this."

'It isn't often that a close friend commits suicide," Peter said.

"Or gets murdered," Searle added.

For the first time since her long glance at him when he had come into the room, Sarah let her gaze dwell upon him. There was something contemptuous in her eyes, as if she found what he had said merely sensational and not at all convincing, but she did not speak. The four of them sat there in silence till Colonel Raven came back into the room.

Harriet was the next to be questioned by Raposo and after her Peter. The detective asked him to be seated, but he himself moved restlessly about the room, pausing here and there apparently to examine some ornament with great intentness, almost as if he were putting a price on it. And perhaps, Peter thought, that was precisely what he was doing. Perhaps he was trying to place the Ravens, to decide to what class they belonged and whether they were rich or poor. To Peter the house suggested genteel poverty, but their foreignness might make it difficult for the chefe to assess this.

But it seemed that Peter had been right that Raposo's thoughts had been on some such matter, for his first question, asked suddenly as he turned to Peter and sat down facing him, was, "Mr. Corey, was Mr. Methven a rich man?"

"He wasn't when I saw him last," Peter answered. "But as I told you, that was a long time ago. I don't know what may have happened since then."

"His home is very agreeable," Raposo said. "The home of a cultured man with comfortable means. I do not suppose that he had financial worries."

"No, I thought that myself," Peter agreed.

"But you know nothing of his financial situation?"

"Nothing at all. As a matter of fact, I know nothing at all about his life here, we've been out of touch for so long."

"Then may I ask what made you want

to resume your relationship all of a sudden?"

Peter had been prepared for his question and had decided to answer it with a partial lie.

"I wanted to come to Madeira for a holiday," he said, "and I happened to know he was living here, so I wrote to him on the chance that he might like to see me and he sent me a very warm invitation to stay with him. Naturally I was very pleased. We were good friends once."

"How did you know he was living here?" Raposo asked.

"His wife's a friend of mine. She told me." That was as much, Peter hoped, as he need say about Clare. The complexity of his relationship with her was something that he did not relish trying to explain to this policeman.

"So he was married," Raposo said.

"Yes, when I knew them first, but they broke up soon after."

"Where was it that you knew them? In England?"

"No, in Hong Kong. Mr. Methven was in the police force there. I was a lecturer in the university.''

"So he was a policeman,'' Raposo said with interest. "But he was not living here on a policeman's pension.''

"No, I shouldn't say he was. And anyway, he didn't stay long in the police, only three years or thereabouts, I think. After that he went to fight in the Congo when there were troubles there and that's when I lost touch with him.''

"He went as a mercenary?''

"I believe so.''

"And before he went to Hong Kong?''

"I believe he was a pilot in an air-taxi company and before that in the R.A.F. He'd had a bad childhood, I know. His parents died young and I think he was brought up by foster parents.''

"Always a man of action, then, and perhaps not very stable. Yet he has been living here very quietly for a number of years. It looks as if at some time his nature underwent a change.''

Peter nodded. "That's how it looks to me.''

"And then, in the end, suicide.''

"I thought you were inclined to think it

might be murder," Peter said.

"I am bearing both possibilities in mind," the detective said composedly. "Tell me, Mr. Corey, what do you think of a theory of mine? I believe that often men who are strongly drawn to lead lives full of action, dangerous, adventurous lives, may actually be courting death. When men are drawn to fighting and killing, it is their own deaths that they seek. They wish to die. Particularly I think this is true when they have no need to do so. In wartime, when there is no choice, it is different, but for someone like your friend only taking risks gave him peace of mind."

Peter looked at the other man with interest. "It's possible. So you think after all he may have been a suicidal type."

"It might be so. But at the same time such men meet many strange people and might well have enemies. But of course you know nothing of that."

"Nothing at all, I'm afraid. And if he really was suicidal for a time, it looks as if he may have outgrown it in recent years."

"Yes, I had thought of that. When did

you leave Hong Kong yourself?"

"About the same time as Mr. Methven. I found I could write fairly profitably and settled in London."

"Ah, you are a writer. Under your own name?"

"Yes."

"I regret I do not know your work."

"I don't think I've ever been translated into Portuguese. In any case, I write mainly for children." Peter was becoming intensely impatient to be asked a certain question and had begun to feel that the chefe was deliberately keeping off it. He introduced the subject himself. "I should tell you, I think, that while we were waiting for you to arrive at Mr. Methven's house, I went wandering around in it, looking for drinks, and accidentally I went into his bedroom. It was in a state of chaos. Someone had searched it, hadn't they?"

He saw a glint in the chefe's melancholy eyes. "So you saw that. Yes, someone searched in a great hurry for something and we do not know for what, whoever he was, or whether or not he found it. And

86

we do not know when it happened, before Mr. Methven's death or after it. If it was after his death, why the hurry? Mr. Methven could not interrupt him. Of course, the man, or it may have been the woman, may have feared that someone else might come — that would explain the haste. And we have to recognise that if the search was before Mr. Methven's death and he caught him, I do not think it could have been a reason for murder. For a man searching as that one was searching, if he killed at all, it would have been swift and violent and we should have found Mr. Methven dead on the floor of his bedroom or in the hall, not comfortably settled in a chair on his patio. So it is not impossible, I think, that that search had nothing to do with his death."

"A bit of a coincidence if it hadn't, surely," Peter said.

"Coincidences happen every day."

"Have you considered the possibility that it was Mr. Methven himself who made the search for something he had lost?"

"And the discovery of his loss led

to his suicide?"

"Not necessarily. As you say, there may have been no connection between it and his death. All the same, what about it?"

"I have considered this, of course," Raposo said in his sombre, quiet way, as if he had already considered many things and found none of them rewarding. "I believe you arrived in Funchal on the same plane as Mr. Searle."

"Yes," Peter replied, not understanding the reason for this sudden switch in the chefe's line of questioning.

"Did you know he was coming here?"

"No, I didn't even know who he was or that he was related to Mr. Methven. In fact, I didn't know that Mr. Methven had a nephew or any relations."

"So when you arrived here, you were not expecting Mr. Searle to arrive here almost immediately after you."

"No. Oh, I see . . ." Suddenly Peter understood the implication of the last few questions. "You're thinking that if I knew he was coming and that at best I'd only a few minutes before he got here, I might have been in a great hurry to make that search myself. However, I didn't, though I don't suppose I can prove it."

"It is only one of the possibilities I have been considering," Raposo said in a tone almost of apology. "I have to consider everything."

"I see that."

"Where are you going to stay tonight?"

"At some hotel."

"It will be easy to find a room. This is not the season for Madeira. May I recommend the Victoria? If you like I will telephone and reserve a room for you. I imagine you do not find it easy to use the telephone here."

"That would be very kind," Peter said.

It would also be practical, he realised, from the chefe's point of view, to be sure where he was going to spend the night, and it did not surprise him at all later, when Michael Searle had been questioned, to discover that he too had had a room obligingly booked for him at the Hotel Victoria.

CHAPTER 6

When they were both about to take their leave from the Ravens' house, the colonel offered to telephone a taxi for them. It arrived in only a few minutes and in only a few minutes delivered them at a towering, white, flood-lit building, where a uniformed porter took charge of their luggage and another of their passports and asked them to register.

Michael Searle looked round him uneasily, as if he was hoping that the place was not as expensive as it looked. There was a great deal of gilt in the entrance hall, a tall mirror that made the hall look even larger than it was, and an immense bowl of flowers, blue agapanthus, milky white arum lilies, roses, and carnations, standing on a marble table in front of the mirror.

Seeing himself in it, looking jaded and unusually pale, Peter suddenly felt far more middle-aged than he generally did, and exhausted and useless. Here he was, involved in something which, he admitted to himself, meant very little to him, because his friendship with Alec Methven had long ago worn itself out, yet unable to extricate himself for he did not know how long.

How much better for him it would have been if he had resisted the pressure that Clare had put on him to come to Madeira and gone off to the Highlands, looking for a new background for the next adventure of Edward Otter. In Scotland otter-hunting was still permitted, he believed, though it was prohibited in England and Wales, and Edward Otter might not be aware of this and so might land himself on a visit to relatives in altogether unexpected dangers. The situation had decided possibilities.

"I don't feel at all like sleep yet,"

Searle said as the porter started towards the lift with their luggage. "What about another drink before we go to bed?"

Peter withdrew his gaze from the weary, ageing face that looked back at him from the mirror and reluctantly relinquished the calming company of Edward Otter.

"I suppose the bar's still open," he said.

"I think you'll find it stays open round the clock here," Searle said.

"All right, then I'll meet you there in a few minutes."

Peter let himself be led away to his room, while Searle was taken to his.

Peter found his pleasantly furnished with an inviting-looking bed in it on to which, he all at once discovered, he would have been delighted to throw himself if he had not agreed to meet Searle in the bar. The curtains at the tall window were drawn. Parting them, he peered out. The window was closed and there was a wire screen beyond it. Opening both the window and the screen, he stepped out on to a small balcony, from which, far below, he could see a faint glitter of reflected light on the surface of the inky sea. The air blowing in from it was refreshingly cool. At some distance he could see the lights of the town, sloping up steeply from a darkness that he took to be the water's edge to another darkness that he thought must be the beginning of the mountains.

He stood there for a few minutes, hearing some night bird make a strange rattling noise in the palms that he could see dimly in the gardens below him, then he turned back into the room, unpacked quickly, and went looking for Searle in the bar.

He was already there, waiting for Peter. There were a few other people there, but voices were quiet and the waiters who came and went among the tables moved softly, needing only a word or a glance to bring what was wanted. In the hush it felt natural to Peter, apart from the fact that what he and Searle had to say to one another was private, that they should speak in lowered voices.

To begin with, indeed, neither appeared to have anything to say. Their table faced a long window from which they could see the same pattern of lights that Peter had seen from his balcony and they sat there for a few minutes, gazing out and sipping their drinks, without speaking.

At last Searle said, "You did say, didn't you, you didn't know Alec had a nephew?"

"I believe I did," Peter answered.

"Of course, if you hadn't seen him for fifteen years, I can understand that," Searle said. "I'd have been only ten then and I never saw much of him till my mother died."

"She was his sister, I think you said."

"Yes, but they didn't get on. They were separated when they were children and really never saw much of one another, even when they grew up."

"I know Alec was brought up by foster parents," Peter said, "but I didn't know anything about his having a sister."

He was too tired to be much interested, but he recognised a great urge to talk in the young man and did not want to show him too blank a face.

"Yes, they were sent to different

families," Searle said. "I don't think it was for any special reason. It was just an administrative bungle. And my mother could never settle down with anyone. They were always saying they couldn't cope with her, so eventually she got dumped in an orphanage and after a little of that she ran away, and that's a part of her life I don't know much about, though I suppose I can guess what it was. She married later and I think her husband was my father, but he didn't stick around for long, I can't remember him. She worked as a waitress till she died, but there were always men around our home and of course I didn't understand what they were doing there until much later, but we weren't too poor. She hardly ever spoke of Alec. I knew she had a brother somewhere, but he never seemed of any importance till one day he turned up to take me away from the foster home I'd been put into. He'd kept enough in touch with my mother to know I existed, and I suppose, as my only relation, he was officially notified of what had happened to me and a foster home seemed to be something he wouldn't wish on his worst enemy, though as a matter of fact I was quite happy where I was. They were nice people who'd taken me on."

"Why were he and your mother put into foster homes in the first place?" Peter asked. "What happened to their parents?"

"My grandfather was a builder's labourer," Searle said. "He drank a great deal and he got violent when he was drunk. He used to knock my grandmother about and one day he killed her. He didn't mean to and when he realised what he'd done, he cut his throat. The two children were alone in the house with them for two days before anyone came to help them. Two days with a couple of corpses." He drank some whisky, then gave a hard little laugh. "I don't come of a very respectable family, do I?"

Peter did not reply at once. It had occurred to him while the young man was talking that he was enjoying telling the story, that probably he had told it often before, embellishing it a little at each telling, and even that it might have no truth in it whatsoever. But if it had, it explained a good deal that Peter had never understood about Alec, his aloofness, his inability to make warm human contacts.

After a pause, he said, "What happened after he took you away from the foster home?"

"Oh, he sent me to school," Searle answered. "A quite expensive boarding school where they took children whose parents were working abroad and where they could stay during the holidays. I don't know that I enjoyed it any more than I'd have enjoyed the home, but at least I had a very good education. Alec was crazy about education. He was very bitter that he'd had next to none himself and had had to make up for it all on his own."

"So he could already afford to send you to a good school," Peter said. "Was that on a mercenary's pay?"

"I don't really know. I don't think he was a mercenary for long, but he had some sort of job out there — in Zaire, as it's called now — and he only came to see me occasionally on short visits to England.

I owed him absolutely everything and I had a kind of hero-worship of him, but I didn't really get to know him till he settled here. When he did that I came to stay with him from time to time. But I must have been pretty much of a disappointment to him. I think I told you, he'd set his heart, when I went to Cambridge, on my turning into somebody learned, and he simply couldn't understand how I could have so little ability and so little interest in that kind of thing.''

"What do you do?" Peter asked.

"I'm an actor," Searle replied. "Rather second rate, as I'm coming to realise, but it's all I've ever wanted to be.''

Peter remembered his first impression in the aeroplane that there was something theatrical about the young man.

"Will you go on with it if you find you've inherited a good deal from Alec?" he asked.

Searle gave him a puzzled look. "A good deal? What do you call a good deal?''

"Well, on top of paying for your education, he wasn't living as a poor man, you know. And you seem to be his only relative.''

''But he hasn't had much money recently, whatever he had once,'' Searle said. ''He couldn't have had. He was earning money giving English lessons to taxi drivers and waiters and people like that.''

''He may have been doing it just for the interest of it.''

''Yes, but you see . . .'' Searle hesitated, his face, which was almost as tired as Peter's, flushing a little. ''I didn't understand it at the time, I just took it for granted, but when he sent me to school and looked after me, I think he deprived himself to do it. He had this thing about education. And he thought of me as a kind of son, you see.''

''I still think he wasn't poor,'' Peter said. ''Somehow he did all right in Zaire. By the way, did you find his will when you were searching his bedroom?''

Searle started violently. His mouth opened as if he were going to say something, then it remained hanging open, as if he had forgotten what he had been about to say. It was a moment before he remarked in a detached tone of voice, "I don't know what you mean."

"Didn't you search his room while I was at the Ravens', getting them to telephone for the police?" Peter asked. "Wasn't that why you wanted me to go to them instead of going yourself? You knew them, so it would have been far better sense for you to go."

"I never knew them well," Searle said. "They aren't my sort. Anyway, I — I felt sort of responsible for Alec and that I ought to stay with him. You must understand, I was very fond of him."

"And you didn't search for anything in his bedroom?"

"I never even went into it. I did look round to see if I could find a letter from him, but not in his bedroom. Why do you think I did?"

"It's something our friend the chefe said to me." Peter had had this thought in his mind for some minutes, but now wondered what had made him bring it up, for even if he was right that Searle had been the searcher, it was certain that he would deny it and there would be no way of proving that he was lying. But having gone so far, it was only reasonable to offer some explanation. "He said it had obviously been a hurried search and that if it had been done immediately after Alec died, there could have been no need for that kind of hurry, but if it was done before his death and he interrupted it, then he wouldn't have been given a chance to die comfortably in that chair on the patio. So that left a rather puzzling situation behind. But later it struck me that if you wanted to search for something in his bedroom and that was why you got rid of me, you'd of course have been in a hell of a hurry. And I still have a certain liking for that explanation."

He was expecting expostulation, denials, anger, and was wondering if in the tone of those things he might not catch some glimpse of the truth. But Searle only turned his face aside, so that he could look out at the lights of Funchal, and observed quietly, "So he believes it was murder."

A second-rate actor he might be, Peter

thought, but one who had great control of both expression and voice.

"Don't you?" he said.

Searle turned back to look at him, giving him one of his sudden, charming smiles. "If it was, then you and I have both got perfect alibis, haven't we? Each of us knows the other was on the plane that came in at seven-thirty, and by that time Alec had been dead for hours. So even if he left me the vast fortune you seem to believe in, I shan't be suspected of having done him in. How I wish that fortune existed! And even if anyone gets the idea I searched his bedroom for something — which, as I said, I didn't — it won't really matter, because it couldn't have had anything to do with his murder. Now I think I'll go to bed. You've got some queer ideas about me, but I don't really blame you. We're all in a queer state tonight. I'll see you sometime in the morning, I expect."

He got to his feet and went out.

Peter stayed on where he was for a little while, taking his time to finish his drink. With Searle's disappearance he stopped thinking about him. He even stopped asking himself if he believed that Alec's death was suicide or murder. It was in the end simply death, and that was that. Peculiarly sad for Peter, because with what he had learnt about Alec that evening, he had begun to seem more interesting than he ever had before. But meanwhile Peter had another matter on his mind. He ought to send a cable to Clare.

He supposed that the hotel porter would see to that for him. Getting up, he made his way back to the entrance hall, told the porter there that he wanted to send a cable, was given a form, then stood looking at it blankly, suddenly finding himself unable to think of a single thing to write.

After a little while he wrote Clare's name and address on the form, then paused again. At last, hesitating between the words, he wrote slowly and carefully, "Arrived here to find Alec dead shot through head probably suicide am remaining here for the present in Hotel Victoria send instructions if any Peter."

103

Did that sound too bald, too brutal? Ought he not to have said something about his deep regrets and his profound sympathy?

No, not to Clare, whose feelings were likely to be only superficially disturbed. He handed the cable to the porter, went to the lift, and as it took him up to his floor, started to wonder if the cable would bring her and whether or not he hoped that it would.

CHAPTER 7

In the morning the sky was a radiant blue with only a faint blur of cloud above the horizon and with a glitter of brilliant light on the calm sea. Peter ordered a breakfast of coffee and rolls and ate it on his small balcony, on which the sunshine was almost too dazzling.

He had slept deeply, but still felt an aching sense of fatigue, which had nothing much to do, he supposed, with actual tiredness, but was a leftover of the strain and distress of the evening before. Yet as he sat with his eyes half-closed against the glare, too indolent to get up and fetch his sunglasses, he found it oddly difficult to remember what had happened.

A vision of Alec dead in his chair was clear in his mind, but the features of the strangers whom he had met, with the exception of the fine-boned face and melancholy eyes of the chefe, were confused and dim. He would see them all again, he was sure, perhaps later that same day, and would sort them out then and come to some conclusions as to the kind of people they were, but for the present he was indifferent to them. He sat there, letting the sunshine soak into him and lull him into an even deeper lethargy.

But at last he got up, shaved, changed out of his pyjamas into his swimming trunks and put on the beach robe that he had brought. He picked up his sunglasses and the Rex Stout that he had started to read on the aeroplane the day before, and took the lift down into what seemed to be the very bowels of the hotel, emerging at the end on the level of the swimming pool.

He would have had to make his way very much farther down through the flowery gardens to reach the sea and this morning he felt too idle to set about it. Choosing a lounging chair near the edge of the pool, he settled back to absorb some more sunshine before taking his first plunge into the water.

He noticed with dissatisfaction how pallid he looked compared with most of the other people there who had had time to acquire a holiday tan, and also that swimming trunks did nothing to conceal the paunch that he was developing. There was rather more of one than he had realised and perhaps it was time, he thought, for him to start trying to do something about it. Not that he would necessarily be successful, even if he made the effort. A middle-aged spread was a stubborn thing, once it had started, and anyway, he had never had any inclination to appear younger than he was. So why should he worry? Opening his book, he let himself enjoy vicariously one of Nero Wolfe's more splendid meals.

A voice nearby interrupted him. "A better morning for a change, thank God! I've hardly seen the sun since I came."

It irritated Peter to be forced to talk. He was not feeling sociable. He said, "That's too bad," and ostentatiously went on reading.

The man who had spoken arranged himself in the chair next to Peter's. He was about fifty, but there was no middle-aged spread about him. He was long and lean, with a look of well-muscled vitality. His hair was grey, but it was thick and curly. With the big dark glasses that masked his eyes it was impossible to make much of his face, except for the friendly mouth, which showed excellent teeth when he smiled.

"Some fool at home sold me the idea that the climate's the same all the year round on Madeira," he said. "When you get here the people who really know the place tell you May and June are the off-season. August and September are the time to come if you really want sunshine. D'you know this island well?"

"I've never been here before," Peter said.

"Staying long?"

"I haven't really decided."

"That's how I like to travel myself. I like to come and go as I choose, not get myself tied up in one of those package deals. Are you here alone?"

Peter was about to say that he was when he remembered Michael Searle. In a sense it might be said that they were here together.

"Well, more or less," he said.

"I'm alone too," the other man said. "That's how I like it. I like my independence. By the way, my name's Frank Pelley."

Peter felt that he had to respond. "Mine's Peter Corey."

Frank Pelley smiled. "To tell the truth, I thought it was. I've some young nieces I give your books to every Christmas, and there's a photograph of you on the jacket. I thought I couldn't be wrong. Hope you don't mind. Now I must have my swim, so I'll leave you in peace to get on with your book."

Standing up, he untied the belt of the white towelling robe that he was wearing and took off from the edge of the pool in a clean dive, then surfaced, doing an elegant crawl.

Puzzled, because the photographs of him that appeared on the jackets of his books were at least ten years out of date and had never been particularly like him, Peter wished that he had been taught to swim like that when he was young. But glad to be relieved of the need to go on making pointless conversation, he resumed his reading.

He went into the pool himself before his neighbour returned. He swam up and down with a laborious breast stroke, wondering how many lengths he would be able to do before the unaccustomed exercise tired him out. In fact, he found it so stimulating that he was able to go on for far longer than he had expected. He could not remember quite how long it was since he had gone swimming last. In Italy, he thought it had been, three or four years ago. It had been stupid, since he had the money for it, to neglect something so enjoyable for so long. It had the wonderful quality of obliterating thought. The shadow left by the evening before faded in the clear, sparkling water. He nearly forgot that it had been the police who had placed him in the Hotel Victoria.

Then all of a sudden he came face to

face with Sarah Baird.

He had noticed her, with only a dim sense of recognition, a moment before, when she had stood poised on the springboard at the deep end of the pool, then had taken off into the water in a beautiful, supple dive. She had looked so different from the girl whom he had seen the evening before that he had made no real effort to connect the two images. It was only when she came up smoothly to the surface just in front of him and pushed her clinging dark hair back from her face, that he was sure who it was.

She recognised him at the same moment.

"Oh, it's you," she said.

She was gently treading water, letting it hold her up with a look of relaxed satisfaction. There was colour in her cheeks and her eyes were bright. Peter wondered why he had not thought her pretty the evening before. She was not outstanding, but she had a quite charming face, particularly when she smiled.

"I'm sorry, I'm afraid I behaved very badly yesterday," she said. "You must have thought I was awful."

"I don't suppose any of us were quite ourselves then," he said.

"After you and Michael left, James really took it out on me for behaving like a moron," she said. "Of course, he hates me."

"James?" For a moment Peter forgot who that was.

"Colonel Raven. You're staying here, I suppose."

"Yes, Mr. Raposo booked me in here last night. D'you often come swimming here?"

"Most days. You can get tickets to come in, if you aren't staying in the hotel. Now I'd like to dive again, but you won't go away, will you? I'd like to talk to you."

"No, I'll be around."

She swam away from him, climbed out of the pool, and went back to the springboard. She was wearing a small scrap of yellow bikini. What it did not cover was a warm, even brown. She was long-legged, flat-breasted, and very bony, but there was a casual grace in the way she moved which was very attractive. Certainly, Peter thought, as he swam towards the shallow end to clamber out of the water, she was one of the people who are much improved by shedding their clothes.

Returning to his chair, he found his talkative neighbour was back again, but appeared to be asleep. He had wrapped himself up against the sun in his white robe and wore his big round glasses. He had become an anonymous figure, featureless and inert. Peter resumed his reading until presently Sarah joined him. She stood over him, towelling her long, dark, dripping hair.

"Of course, James is quite right about me," she said. "I *am* a bit mental. You saw that yourself last night. And he's longing for me to leave."

Peter made room for her at the end of his chair. "Why don't you, then?"

"Because of Harriet," she said as she sat down beside him. "I think she needs me."

"It was my impression that it was you who needed her."

"Well, these things are generally mutual, aren't they? We depend on each other a lot. She needs a daughter to look after and I need a mother — or I suppose I do. Everyone seems to think so. I've never had one of my own that I can remember, so I don't quite know. But she was my mother's best friend and when she died Harriet helped my father a lot, looking after me. I sometimes think it was a pity she didn't marry him instead of James."

"Why didn't she?"

"I don't think he ever asked her. He'd been terribly in love with my mother and when she died he gave everything left over in the way of love to me. I believe I look rather like her."

It occurred to Peter that, just as she had the night before, the girl had immediately made herself the centre of the conversation. But he was interested in her and encouraged her.

"Was Mrs. Raven in love with him?" he asked.

"I'm not quite sure," she said. "It's the sort of thing she'd never talk about.

Anyway, she met James in the hospital where they operated on his knee — she was a nurse then — and they got married soon afterwards."

"What's she so afraid of?" Peter asked.

The girl's eyebrows went up. "Afraid?"

"Yes, she's got such frightened eyes. She looked frightened all yesterday evening."

She shook her head. "That's just her shyness. She's terribly shy. I know that's funny for a nurse, because she can't afford to be shy on her job, but I suppose that's different. But she isn't afraid of anything, not even of James when he gets into a temper, and that often frightens me. He's got a wicked temper. I think it's horrible, but she doesn't seem to mind."

"Perhaps she understands him better than you do."

"Yes, of course she does. But why should I try to understand him when he doesn't try to understand me? He thinks I ought to go away and get a job. But why should I do that when I've got enough money to live on? It would only be taking the job away from someone who really needs it."

"Isn't there anything you're interested in?" he asked. "Wouldn't it help you to have an occupation of some sort, even if it's one you aren't paid for?"

"Oh, good works!" she said contemptuously. "I don't think that's my line."

"You might study something," he suggested. "You might go to a university. Wouldn't that be better than spending your time with two middle-aged people?"

He was surprised to see that she seemed to shrink away from him.

"I like them much better than people of my own age," she muttered in a sullen tone, "who bore me terribly. Besides, I told you, Harriet needs me. She will all the more now that Alec's dead. She'll be dreadfully lonely here."

"Then were she and Alec close friends?"

"Oh yes. I used sometimes to wonder if they were lovers. Is it awful of me to say that? But actually I don't think they were. She's always been much too loyal to James, though he really isn't worth it."

She made this statement in an almost clinical tone of detachment.

Peter wondered if she had been jealous of her godmother's friendship with Alec.

"You were very fond of Alec yourself, weren't you?" he said.

She gave a grave nod. "Oh yes, after my father and Harriet, I've never been so fond of anyone. He was a really good man. He was generous and gentle and he never tried to push me around and make me do things I didn't want to. It was horrible that he had to die."

Peter picked up her phrase quickly. "How do you mean, *had* to die?"

"Well, you don't commit suicide unless you're absolutely driven to it, do you?" she said, looking as if she found it strange that he had not understood her. "I mean, you don't say to yourself one day, 'Now what shall I do this afternoon, play golf or shoot myself? Come to think of it, I believe I'll shoot myself.' You only do it if you feel you've absolutely got to, that you've no choice." She added darkly, "I know what I'm talking about."

He waited for her to go on, but it

seemed that she had said all that she meant to say.

"Yes, I see," he said. "Of course, you're right. But have you any idea of your own why he did it?"

"If I'd known anything about it, I'd have done my best to stop it, shouldn't I?" she said. "I don't think anyone will ever be able to explain it. He didn't want us to, did he? If he had, he'd have left a letter behind. Now what do you feel about lunch? One can get a buffet lunch on the terrace just down those steps over there. I often have it when I've been here swimming. Would you like that?"

Peter replied that a buffet lunch was a very good idea, picked up his belongings, and followed Sarah down the steps to the terrace below.

She came as she was, in her bikini, with her damp hair falling about her shoulders. On the terrace there were a number of small tables and a long counter from which they could help themselves to food. They had sandwiches made of some smoked pink fish that was faintly reminiscent of smoked salmon, fresh apricots, and coffee, and chose a table in the shade of a tall palm. The shade was welcome to Peter, who was beginning to feel a tingling on his skin which he thought would probably develop into soreness. He had been foolish to expose his unaccustomed body to the sun for as long as he had that morning.

Bony and unexpectedly appealing, Sarah arranged her brown limbs at the table, one elbow on it and her head on her hand.

"I told you Alec lent me one of your books, didn't I?" she said. "Tell me, why do you write about otters? Do you know an awful lot about them?"

"I don't know anything at all," he said. "I'm sure if I'd ever been intimate with a real otter, I couldn't write my fairy tales about them."

"What made you pick on them, then?"

"Perhaps because they're a threatened species. It gave me a sense of kinship."

"D'you think we're threatened, then?"

"Well, aren't we?"

"Of course, Edward Otter's really yourself, isn't he?"

"Oh no, I'm not nearly so ingenious

119

or courageous."

"But you'd like to be."

"Well, naturally."

"Perhaps you would be if you were tested," she said. "Have you ever been tested?"

She was studying him with bright, inquiring eyes. She looked cheerful and interested, not in the least as if she had had a brush with death the evening before and lost a friend to whom she was said to have been devoted.

"Never very seriously," Peter answered. "But one can know a good deal about one's own limitations without actually putting them to the test."

"I don't think one can," she said. "I keep taking myself by surprise. I hardly ever know in advance how I'm going to feel about things. But perhaps that means I haven't much imagination. What do you think?"

He noticed that she had brought the talk round to herself again.

"Perhaps you'll do better after a little more practice," he said. "One needs some experience."

"For instance," she said, "when my father died . . . ."

But there she broke off. Her expression changed completely. It had been open and unself-conscious. Now, all of a sudden, it was cold and withdrawn.

Peter realised that Michael Searle had approached them and was standing just behind his chair, holding a plate of sandwiches and a glass of wine. He was wearing swimming trunks and a loose, brightly patterned shirt.

"Mind if I join you?" he said.

Sarah did not reply. She turned her head away and seemed to be studying something far out to sea. Michael did not wait for anyone to answer his question but sat down at the table. Her rigid silence made an impression on him. Catching Peter's eye, he looked at him with raised eyebrows. Peter responded with a faint shrug.

Michael bit into a sandwich. After a moment he said, "Sarah, d'you know I sometimes get the feeling you've really forgotten me? Or else that you think I've done some frightful thing. What is it?

Can't we be friends as we used to be?"

He put all the charm of which he was capable into his voice, watching her with an unusual look of anxiety on his round, amiable face.

She said nothing, but instead stood up quietly, smiled at Peter, and walked away. She had eaten only half of her sandwiches and had not touched her apricots.

"Well, I'm damned," Michael muttered. "Have I a bad smell or something?"

"It looks as if her memory of you can't be altogether pleasant," Peter said. "You seem to have done something to upset her."

"She's just nuts," Michael said. "Isn't she supposed to have had a breakdown of some kind?"

"So Mrs. Raven said."

"Perhaps it's left her with a phobia about the colour of my eyes or something. Pity, she rather appeals to me. She isn't ordinary. But disentangling her would be quite a job, wouldn't it? Beyond me, I expect. I'm sorry I spoilt your lunch, but I didn't expect her to react like that." With a frown on his face as if it mattered to him a good deal, he added, "Well, to hell with her — it doesn't matter."

CHAPTER 8

Peter spent most of the afternoon on his balcony, which was in shade now, dozing. His swimming had made him very sleepy. He would have liked to get in touch with the chefe to ask him how long he thought it would be necessary for him to stay, not because of any great urge that he felt to get away from his pleasant surroundings, but because he was beginning to find it impossible to settle down here and enjoy them or ignore them.

He did not feel as if he were on a holiday, yet he could not work either. If he had been at home and had become involved in some such calamity as he had here, he would certainly have taken refuge in work. A whole new story about Edward Otter might have come out of it. But here there was no distraction but pleasure, and he did not feel in the mood for that. He thought it would only irritate the detective to be pursued, though it would be easy enough to telephone him from the hotel, where some English-speaking employee would put him through to the *policia*. He was considering this uncertainly when he was acutely startled by the sudden ringing of the telephone in his room.

Going in from the balcony, he picked up the telephone, sure that the caller would be the chefe. But it was Harriet Raven.

In a nervous voice, as if she was afraid that she might be doing something tactless, or even improper, she said, "Mr. Corey, if you aren't doing anything else, would you care to have drinks with us this evening?"

"That's very kind of you," he said. "I'd like it very much."

"It's just that we thought you might be feeling — well, rather lost in the circumstances," she said.

"I am," he answered.

"We all are, of course. But as you're alone, we thought . . ." She hesitated. "But if you prefer being alone — I mean, if talking to strangers doesn't appeal to you at the moment — please just say so. We'll understand."

"I'll be grateful for your company," he said.

"If you're sure, then. It's difficult to know how another person will feel, what it's best to do, but we thought . . ." She hesitated again, but this time, in her desperate uncertainty of herself, did not go on.

"I don't much like being alone at the moment," he tried to reassure her. "I'll look forward to seeing you again."

"Good. About six o'clock then. I don't expect you know the way, so I'd take a taxi. There's no town in the world with quite so many taxis as Funchal. Or shall I fetch you? Yes, I'll fetch you. It'll only take me a few minutes to drive down."

"No, no, I'll take a taxi," he said.

But she had taken it into her head that it was her duty to fetch him and it took him a little while to persuade her that a taxi would suit him very well. She was one of those people who find it very difficult to end a telephone conversation. When she finally did, he looked at his watch. It was four o'clock. That left him plenty of time for another swim. Changing back into his swimming trunks, he went down once more to the pool.

But his afternoon swim was not as agreeable as the one in the morning, because the bank of cloud which in the morning had been only a smudge along the horizon had edged up over most of the sky, had become as overcast as the evening before. A little breeze was blowing which felt almost chilly on his skin. He stayed in the pool for only a few minutes and did not linger beside it afterwards. Going back to his room, he put on the only good suit that he had brought and settled down to read until it was time to go to the Ravens'.

Harriet greeted him at the gate as he paid off his taxi. She was in another lightly flowing dress, very like the one that she had worn the evening before, except that this one was of flame colour. In the daylight he saw that there was a small garden in front of the pale blue house, with a jacaranda in bloom beside the gate and spiky agaves on either side of the path that led up to the front door. Harriet glanced up and down the street as if she was looking for someone, then led Peter into the house.

"I'm sorry, James is out on his walk," she said, "but he'll be back any time now. He's been told he should try to go for a walk every day, or his joints will simply seize up. He's very brave about it, because actually he finds walking quite painful."

She led him through the living room on to the small patio. She had drinks there waiting on a low cane table and gestured to him to sit down on one of the cane chairs. When she had poured out whisky for him and a gin and tonic for herself, she sat down facing him. In the garden behind the house there were rose bushes, rich clumps of carnations, and a small, well-kept lawn. They gave it almost the character of an English garden.

"Sarah told me she had lunch with you," she said. "She's lying down now, but she'll come down presently, I expect. She's taken a liking to you. She'll want to see you.''

"She doesn't seem to have taken a liking to poor Michael Searle,'' Peter said. "She and I were getting along very nicely, I thought, but as soon as he joined us she left us without a word.''

She gave a sad little smile. "That's only because he's young. She prefers us middle-aged people. She feels safer with us. It's a leftover from her breakdown and something to do with losing her father so suddenly, and at the moment losing Alec seems to have brought it all back just when I thought she was beginning to get over it.''

"She seemed quite bright and cheerful when I saw her this morning until Michael came along,'' Peter said, "though I remember she did seem to recoil when I suggested she might think of going to a university.''

"Yes, that's just it, you see,'' she said. "I've made the same suggestion myself. She's got her A levels and so on. I'm sure she could get into one. But a university would be full of young people of her own age and she won't face them.''

"Has she always been like that?" Peter asked.

"Oh no! If you'd seen her when she stayed with us two years ago! She was completely different, so friendly with everyone, so full of life! But I suppose there was always some instability there, or she wouldn't have reacted as she has. It wasn't just the death of her father that caused the trouble. She had some sort of unhappy love affair. She won't talk about it much, but I think she thought she was going to get married, then the man ditched her just after her father died, and suddenly she was quite alone. So she took an overdose of sleeping pills. I'm not sure if it was a real attempt, because she didn't take so very many and they pulled her round quite easily in the hospital. Then I was sent for as I was the only person she wanted to see and when I saw the state she was in, quite withdrawn and sometimes just staring straight in front of her for hours, I brought her out here. James thinks it was a mistake and that she ought to have been made to stand on her own feet straightaway, rather like being sent up again in an aeroplane when you've had a crash, but I couldn't bear the thought that the next time she took an overdose it might be more than enough."

Peter thought of the girl saying that you don't commit suicide unless you have no choice. It had not sounded then as if there had been any dark experience in her own life.

"She seems rather young to have had her life blighted by a single unhappy love affair," he said. "I expect she'll get over it."

"Then d'you think we're wrong, letting her stay here?" Harriet asked, her bright dark eyes intently on his, as if his answer might be important. She had the faculty of making everything that he said to her seem important.

"Ah, I hardly know her or any of you," he said. "I think, if anything's wrong, it's perhaps that you worry too much."

"Well, of course I know I do," she said. "And I talk about her too much.

I'm sorry, it's probably fearfully boring. But there was a time when I thought I'd go in for nursing the mentally handicapped and it's always had a great interest for me. Then I got married instead.''

He thought that there was a hint of regret in her voice.

''Do you miss your work?'' he asked.

''Sometimes,'' she admitted. ''If we'd stayed in England I could have gone on with it, but James was sure that the climate here would help him, so we came out one winter and stayed. I'm not sure whether or not it's really helped him and I often think I'd like to go home, but it would be too late to go back to my old job. If I was alone I could do private nursing, but not of course with him to look after. So it's probably best to stay here.''

''And it seems you've got two patients to look after. Perhaps that helps.''

He had not meant to say it seriously, but she greeted it with a troubled frown.

''Then d'you think I'm really keeping Sarah here for my own sake?'' she asked.

"If I thought that, I'd send her away tomorrow. She's got plenty of money, she could look after herself. A grandaunt of hers died about six months ago and left her all she had, which wasn't exactly a fortune, but was a good deal more than most of us have got. And James thinks that's been a calamity, because work is what she needs. I'm not sure myself it's as simple as that. If she weren't successful in whatever she took on, it might finish her off. She needs some kind of success very badly to counterbalance the feeling she's got that nobody cares about her."

"But she must know that you care about her a great deal," Peter said.

"But I'm a woman. I'm really thinking of men. That's where Alec was so marvellous. He was immensely patient with her and I think managed to make her feel that she was really important to him. But there I go again, talking about Sarah. I must try to control it. But I can't discuss her with James, you see, because he just gets irritated, though I know he's very fond of her in his own way." Leaning forward, she took Peter's glass from him and refilled it. "I could discuss her with Alec," she went on, "I could discuss anything with him. He was so understanding and so experienced, he'd known so many different kinds of people and seen so much of the world. And I think he'd been through his own bad times too. I don't know how I'm going to bear it here without him."

From the doorway of the living room a harsh voice said, "You'll find a substitute." Colonel Raven limped forward and sat down stiffly on one of the cane chairs on the patio. He turned a blank, rather unpleasant stare on Peter, who had stood up quickly when he appeared. "Sit down, sit down and go on. Don't let me interrupt anything."

Harriet said, "We were just discussing Sarah."

"Of course, what else?" her husband said sourly. "Mr. Corey, let me warn you, my wife uses that wretched girl and her problems as an introduction to all and sundry, as some people use their pet dogs. You'll have seen that, the dogs start smelling each other and in two shakes the owners are talking like old friends. Well, Sarah's my wife's pet dog. I'm just telling you this because you may not realise what a little sympathy may get you into."

"James — please!" Harriet said.

"Well, it's the truth, isn't it?" the colonel said. "You need people round you all the time. A sick old man like me isn't sufficient. You just ate Alec up and you'll eat Mr. Corey up if he stays around long enough for you to get your hooks into him. Which he won't, if he's got any sense."

Peter had remained standing. He finished his drink and put his glass down. He tried not to let his furious embarrassment show in his face.

"Thank you for the drink, Mrs. Raven," he said. "I enjoyed our talk, but now I think I'd better get back to the hotel."

"Come again, come again!" the colonel exclaimed ironically. "My wife's friends are always welcome."

"Thank you," Peter said gravely, and turned towards the door. "Good evening."

Harriet followed him into the house, then led the way to the front door.

Opening it, she said with agitation, "Please don't take any notice of my husband. He doesn't really mean any of it. It's just that he's in pain. Please — please don't take any notice of it. You really will be welcome if you'll come again. How are you going to get back to the hotel? Shall I call a taxi?"

"I'll walk," Peter said. "I think I know the way now."

He was just about to step out of the house when Sarah appeared at the head of the stairs.

"Oh, are you going already?" she said with dismay. She came quickly down the stairs and looked into her godmother's face. "Something's happened, hasn't it, and I bet I know what."

"Never mind about that now," Harriet said. "Good-bye, Mr. Corey."

Startled and confused by what had happened, but glad to be out of the house with its problems and its conflicts, Peter set off down the road.

Dusk was just beginning to dim the light

of the evening. He found his way back to the Victoria without any difficulty, had another drink at the bar, then dined early. He felt a great deal of sympathy for Harriet Raven, tied to her aggressive and domineering husband, but he hoped that he would not have to expose himself to the same sort of rudeness again. Ending his meal with strawberries, he left the restaurant and was on his way to the lounge to order coffee when he met Michael Searle, going towards the restaurant.

"Hallo," Michael said. "I tried looking for you and telephoning your room to see if you felt like a drink before dinner, but you didn't seem to be around."

"I'm sorry," Peter said. "I was invited to drinks by the Ravens and went. Unluckily it turned out a mixed pleasure."

"They didn't invite me." The corners of Michael's mouth drooped, giving his round face the look of an unhappy child's. "D'you think that girl's put them off me?"

"It seems quite likely," Peter answered.

"She hates the sight of me, doesn't she?

I wonder if one can get over a thing like that, or if it'd just be best to forget her."

"I feel rather inclined to advise you to forget her anyway," Peter said, "or if you're really interested in her, proceed with a certain caution. I don't think she's quite got her feet on the ground."

"That's one of the things I like about her. It makes a change. But I'm sure you're right, caution's the thing." With a smile, as if he had no intention of being taken seriously, Michael went on to the restaurant.

Peter continued on his way to the lounge.

Next morning, as he had the day before, he had breakfast on his balcony, but today there was no sunshine. A sharp wind was blowing, and angry-looking clouds scudded across the sky. In the gardens below the palm trees rattled their fronds. It was not really very pleasant on the balcony, but since he had started his breakfast there, he finished it, then returned to his room, wondering whether to swim or whether the weather made the thought of that too uninviting. But if he did not swim, what was he to do with himself? Walk into Funchal, perhaps, and do a little exploring?

He did not have to solve this problem. It was solved for him. The telephone rang and a voice told him that the senhor chefe wished to speak to him. After a moment Raposo came on the line.

"Good morning, Mr. Corey," he said. "I am in the home of your friend, Mr. Methven. It would oblige me very much if you would join me here."

"Certainly," Peter answered. "As soon as I can."

"I have sent a police car for you," the chefe said. "The agente will bring you."

"Thank you. But may I ask, does this mean you've discovered something about Mr. Methven's death?"

"Yes, we have discovered that it was murder."

"Murder? You sound very sure."

"Yes, we are sure. I believe you have a saying that it is impossible to make an omelet without breaking eggs. This, however, is what someone appears to have done and I do not think it was

139

Mr. Methven."

"I'm afraid I don't understand you," Peter said irritably, feeling that this was not the time for whimsicality.

But the chefe's voice was grave as he went on, "I mean just what I have said. I will explain when you arrive here. It is very simple."

CHAPTER 9

"It is very simple," the chefe repeated when Peter arrived at Alec Methven's house, which had subtly changed its character since he had been in it last. It was almost as if it had become some kind of laboratory, in which nobody could ever have lived. He and the chefe were sitting in the living room.

"And it is no joke that I made about the eggs," the chefe said. "A post-mortem on Mr. Methven's body has shown that only just before his death he consumed an omelet, or eggs in some form, yet a most careful search of his dust bin, which had been emptied only that morning and had next to nothing in it, and also of the rest of the house and even of the garden, has revealed no eggshells. So someone appears to have achieved the impossible. He has made an omelet without breaking eggs.''

''And since you know that that is an impossible thing to do,'' Peter said, ''what do you believe happened?''

The chefe gave a little shrug of his shoulders. His fine-boned face looked tired this morning. There were smudges of shadow under his eyes. But his light blue suit was as spruce as ever and his cheeks were as carefully shaved. He made Peter think of the kind of doctor who, called out to an urgent case in the middle of the night, would not dream of appearing on the scene except in a clean shirt and well-pressed trousers.

''I have spoken to Mr. Methven's maid, Angela,'' the chefe said. ''She came in to clean the house on three mornings a week, but did not do the cooking for him. He preferred to cook for himself and frequently made himself omelets. In the normal way, he would have put the eggshells in the dust bin. She had no suggestion to offer as to why he did not do so on the day of his death, but at least we learnt from her that it must have been after his lunch that he was killed, not after his breakfast, since she came in to clean that morning and he was alive and well when she left at twelve o'clock. Further, she says that he never had anything but coffee and a roll for breakfast. So we can suppose that at least he cooked his lunch as usual, then was killed immediately afterwards."

"How can you be so certain it was immediately after his meal that he was killed?" Peter asked. "Can you pin-point it as exactly as that?"

"In this case, yes, because he had not even begun to digest the food in his stomach," Raposo answered. "I believe that he went straight from the table to the chair on the patio, perhaps to have coffee, and was shot immediately."

"So you think someone had lunch with him here and cleared up afterwards," Peter said.

"That is my theory." The chefe spoke diffidently, as if to have a theory at all was on the daring side. "I believe some acquaintance had lunch with him here and that Mr. Methven made omelets for them both; then they went out to the patio and his visitor shot him. Then he tried to remove the evidence that he had ever been here, washing the dishes and putting them away, leaving everything as if Mr. Methven had had lunch by himself. But the eggshells faced him with a problem. There would have been too many for just one omelet. There would have been the shells of at least four eggs, perhaps more, if the omelets had been large ones, and in an almost empty dust bin they would have been conspicuous. So he decided to remove them from the house, thinking there was less chance of this being noticed than a too large collection of shells. And indeed it was only by chance that it was noticed. It was the woman Angela who pointed it out, her mind being naturally occupied with such things."

"But you'd have realised that without the missing eggshells," Peter said. "The undigested egg in Mr. Methven's stomach would have told you. It can't be normal for suicides to sit down, eat a good meal, wash up tidily, then shoot themselves. I know there are those stories about the condemned man eating a hearty meal before he was hanged, but I can't see a suicide doing it. It looks to me as if your murderer is a fairly ignorant sort of chap, who didn't realise what you'd be able to learn from a post-mortem."

"Not necessarily, no," the chefe answered. "The undigested egg alone would not have told us much. It might not mean that Mr. Methven killed himself immediately after eating. It could have happened hours later. In cases of suicide, where the subject has been under an immense emotional strain while he worked himself up to the act, it is often found that digestion has been almost totally inhibited. Undigested food has been found in the stomach from meals eaten as much as two days before the death. But the missing eggshells indicate clearly that someone was here with Mr. Methven during his lunch, and as he was not expecting to die and so was not in a state of emotional disturbance, we may assume that his digestive processes would have been normal, so that the egg in his stomach tells us that he died immediately after the meal. However, he did not eat alone.''

"You're talking as if the murderer was a man,'' Peter said. "Have you any evidence of that?''

"Ah no, there I made a mistake. I know my knowledge of your language is not perfect. I meant a man or a woman. Which it was we do not know. Perhaps it was more likely to be a woman, to have thought of such a matter as eggshells. But some man might think of it, for instance a professional, trained to think of such details.''

"A professional killer, do you mean?''

"Exactly.''

"But if Mr. Methven had lunch with him, it suggests he was a friend. Are you suggesting he may have had friends among the criminal classes?''

Again Raposo gave his faint shrug. "We still know so little about him. We do not know what is possible.''

"Is that why you asked me up here this morning?'' Peter asked. "To see if

I can give you any information about him?"

"Any information you can give us will be welcome," Raposo said. "But no, it was for another reason."

"You can't want my alibi. You know I hadn't even arrived in Madeira at the time Mr. Methven was killed."

Raposo nodded. "That is correct. We have checked it at your hotel, where they still have your passport. You and Mr. Searle were both on the flight that arrives here at seven-thirty. My wishing to see you, however, was for a quite different reason. I believe when you had discovered Mr. Methven's body and were here in this house with Mr. Searle, Colonel Raven, and Mrs. Raven, you left this room, looking for drinks."

"Yes, and I blundered into Mr. Methven's bedroom, where it was obvious, as I told you, that someone had been searching for something."

"Yes, and then you went on, looking for the drinks, and you found them where?"

Peter looked at him, puzzled, unable

to see where this line of questioning was leading.

"In the dining room," he said.

"And you went in and picked up the tray of drinks and brought it in here?"

Peter nodded.

"Now tell me, please," the chefe said, "when you were in the dining room, do you remember noticing a writing table?"

Peter half-closed his eyes, trying to visualize the room as he had seen it on that one occasion.

"Vaguely," he said.

"Did you happen to notice a small china tray on that writing table, filled with pencils, paper clips, and so on?"

"No, I didn't notice anything like that."

"So you cannot tell me if there was a key on that tray, with a small piece of red ribbon attached to it?"

"No, I'm afraid not."

"Please try very hard to remember. Are you sure you did not see it?"

"I'm not sure that it wasn't there. I'm only sure I didn't notice it."

"Ah . . ." Raposo gave a sigh. "I was afraid that was how it would be. But the woman Angela tells us that a key with a piece of red ribbon tied to it was always there. Ever since she has been working here, and that is now three years, it has been there. She never knew what it was the key to, but she thinks perhaps it was a spare key to this house. And now it is gone. And you see, last night someone entered this house and searched once more. This time searched carefully and methodically. There are no signs of haste. Also there are no signs of breaking in. Whoever came in came either with a key, or else was a very skilled burglar."

"That professional you were talking about."

"Possibly."

"Or someone who took that key from the dining room and let himself in with it."

"Just so."

Peter looked thoughtfully at the neat, quiet man. "Now I think I see where I come in," he said. "You want to know if Searle or either of the Ravens went to the dining room during the time we were waiting for the police to arrive. Could they have taken the key before you got here?"

"That is what I was about to ask," Raposo agreed.

"Well, none of them went to the dining room while I was here," Peter said. "But as you know, Searle was here by himself for a time while I was over at the Ravens', getting them to telephone the police. He could easily have helped himself to the key then. Actually it occurred to me that he might have been the person who searched Mr. Methven's bedroom. If he were, it would account for the haste, wouldn't it? He knew I'd be back in a few minutes. And I challenged him about it later in the evening, but he denied it, as of course he would in any case, whether he'd made the search or not. On the other hand, if he'd a key to the house and knew he could get in when he liked, would he have taken the risk of making that frantic search when he knew he'd hardly any time for it?"

"It seems to me unlikely," Raposo said. "Furthermore, the two searches were entirely different in character. The first one was wild and hurried. The one last night was almost as skillful as a police search would be. Very few things were disturbed. If Angela had not been able to assure us that some of Mr. Methven's shirts were folded differently from how he would have left them, and that some flour had been spilled in one of the kitchen cupboards, showing that someone had been sifting through the flour, and that a few other things were wrong, we might not have noticed anything."

"Angela appears to be a treasure of a witness," Peter said. "The murderer can't have counted on having someone like her around."

The chefe nodded seriously. "Yes, indeed, she has been very helpful."

"I remember your saying the other evening that perhaps the search and the murder were not connected," Peter said. "What do you think about this second search?"

"In character it is a little more like the murder," Raposo answered. "Tidy and careful. It might well be the work of the person who could sit down to lunch with a friend, shoot him, then wash up the dishes and dispose of the eggshells. The first search does not fit in with such a pattern of behaviour."

"Have you any idea what these people were searching for?"

As he asked the question it occurred to Peter that it was unlikely that the chefe would tell him anything, even if he knew the answer. But he showed no signs of evasiveness as he replied, "Not for money or guns, that is all we know. A considerable sum in escudos was left in Mr. Methven's wallet, and we found a revolver in a drawer in the writing table in the dining room."

"A revolver?" Peter said. "He had two, then, the one he was killed with and this other."

"So it would seem. They date, no doubt, from the time you told me of, when he went to fight in the Congo."

"Yes, that seems probable. But if it wasn't money or the second gun that the searcher was after, what did he want? It can't have been anything very large if he thought it might be concealed in a bin of flour."

The chefe stroked one side of his smooth jaw. "I have had one thought about that — only a thought. I have no evidence of it, but first I would like to be sure. It is my impression that you, an old friend, were surprised to find Mr. Methven as affluent as he appears to have been. You were expecting to find him in poverty, and you found not a rich man, but one in very comfortable circumstances. Is that correct?"

Peter nodded.

"So he possessed something which provided him with a good income," Raposo went on, "but which he kept secret. And one of the possessions that has provided many people with good incomes is information. Does it seem to you possible that Mr. Methven could have been living on blackmail?"

An instant denial sprang to Peter's lips. But before speaking, he had second thoughts. What did he actually know of the man who had been living here on Madeira, who seemed in many ways so different from the one whom he had known in Hong Kong?

He replied cautiously, "It would surprise me very much."

Raposo looked as if he had expected no other answer, but he said, "It fits very well, you understand. The blackmailer's victim kills him, arranges the suicide, then makes a search through the house for whatever it was that Mr. Methven held over him, but fails to find it. Later you and Mr. Searle arrive and while you are over at Colonel Raven's house, calling the police, Mr. Searle, knowing of the existence of this object from his uncle — perhaps it is a picture, or letters, or some other document — makes a frantic search for it, hoping to be able to make some profit out of it, as his uncle did. Then last night the first searcher, the tidy man, who has the key, returns and searches again. This time he may have been successful, or he may have been too late, because Mr. Searle already had this object, whatever it was."

"Have you asked him about it?" Peter asked.

A rather sardonic smile lit up the chefe's earnest face. "It is not always useful to ask such a question directly," he said. "In any case, I am only theorizing. It is a habit of mine. I may be wrong from start to finish —" He broke off as an agente came into the room, saying something in Portuguese.

Raposo nodded and the man withdrew.

"It is Colonel Raven," Raposo said. "He wishes to see me."

"I'll go, then, shall I?" Peter said.

"No, wait a little. Let us see what he wants."

Raposo got to his feet and went to the door to meet the colonel.

CHAPTER 10

He came limping in, leaning on his stick.
Seeing Peter, he gave him a quite friendly
nod, as if, at their last meeting, he had
not been bent on insulting him.

"Good morning, Senhor Chefe," he
said. "There seems to be a lot going on
here. I came over to find out what's been
happening. I shouldn't have expected to
see a lot of police around two days after a
suicide. It's murder then, is it?"

"We have fairly conclusive proof of it,"
the chefe replied. "If you had not come
here, I should shortly have come to see
you, to ask a few questions. Perhaps you
can help us."

"We'll all be glad to do anything we

can," the colonel said. "But what's this proof of yours?"

Once more the chefe embarked on an explanation of why undigested egg in Alec Methven's stomach, together with an absence of eggshells, indicated murder.

While he was speaking the colonel lowered himself into a chair, holding the crook of his stick in both hands and leaning his chin on it.

"I see, I see," he said at intervals. Then when the chefe had finished, he remarked, "So he died about the middle of the day and you'll be wanting all our alibis." He turned to Peter. "Yours is straightforward, of course. You were in the aeroplane."

"Actually in London," Peter said. "My flight didn't leave Heathrow till four-ten. But I don't think there's any way I could have managed to be here at lunch time. And the same goes for Searle."

"Well, I had lunch at home with my wife," the colonel said to Raposo. "I don't know if you accept a wife's word as evidence, but it's the best I can do. We had a drink together about twelve-thirty, then lunch about one, then I lay down for a while — I went to sleep for a bit, I think — then we had a cup of tea together as usual about four o'clock, and I went for my walk. I always try to go for a short walk every day. The doctor told me I must. He said I'd soon be stuck in a wheel chair if I didn't. But you aren't interested in anything as late in the afternoon as that, are you? Mind you, the times I've mentioned are only approximate. I didn't expect to be asked to account for my actions and wasn't keeping a check on them."

"Naturally," Raposo said. "But this drink you had before your lunch, you think that was at about twelve-thirty, do you?"

"Round about then," Colonel Raven replied.

"May I ask what you were doing before that?" Raposo asked. "We do not know for certain how early Mr. Methven may have eaten his lunch. We only know he was alive at twelve o'clock, when his maid Angela left him."

"Yes, I understand. Let me see." The colonel screwed up his features as he made an effort to remember. "I was in my study, writing letters, paying bills, and so forth. Those damn bills, how they accumulate! And with the pound on the slide, money goes nowhere. Coming out here on an army pension wasn't the best idea we ever had. All my fault too. My wife wanted to settle in a cottage in Dorset, where she grew up and where she could have got work in the local hospital — she's a splendid nurse, you know, very highly qualified — and her earnings would have helped us quite a bit. But that's beside the point. I was dealing with those bills and things for about an hour, I think."

"Did your wife, or anyone else, come in while you were doing it?"

"I don't remember. Perhaps she did. No, she didn't. And if you want to know what I was doing before about eleven-thirty, I was in my dressing gown on our patio, reading the *Times*. We get it a day late, of course, but I always read it after breakfast. I have my breakfast pretty late as a rule — I've nothing special to get up for — and I don't hurry over it. I sleep very badly and I find it pretty difficult to get going in the mornings. My wife certainly saw me there, if that's what you're going to ask me next."

"What about Miss Baird?" Raposo said. "You have not mentioned her. Did she not have lunch with you?"

"Not lunch, no, I think she'd gone off swimming. She often does that, at the Victoria, then she has her lunch at the buffet there. But you'd better ask her that yourself."

"Did you see her at all during the morning?"

Again the colonel dug his chin into his fingers, as if this helped him to think. "I can't say I remember it. But I don't take much notice of her comings and goings. She'd had breakfast before I had mine, as she always does, I do remember that. But why don't you come over to the house with me and put your questions to her direct? Not that I'm sure if she's in the house now. She may have gone off swimming already. But at least you'll find my wife at home."

"Thank you," Raposo said. "I was

about to suggest that myself."

"And you, Corey?" Colonel Raven said. "Come over and have a drink, or is it too early in the day for you?"

It was earlier than Peter usually had his first drink of the day, but if the colonel was disposed to act as if the evening before had never happened, he was prepared to go along with it. He muttered thanks for the invitation and the three men crossed the road to the blue house opposite.

Colonel Raven opened the door and stood still in the middle of the hall, calling out, "Harriet!"

She emerged from the kitchen, wearing jeans and a white shirt, with her silvery hair, hanging down her back, tied back from her face with a scrap of black ribbon. She gave Peter a bewildered look, as if she could not understand what he was doing there with her husband.

He said, "Where's that girl, Harriet? Is she at home? The senhor chefe wants to question you and her."

"I think she's here," she answered. She stood at the bottom of the stairs and called up them, "Sarah!"

After a moment the girl came to the head of the stairs. Her appearance was startling. She was in a long black hooded garment made of towelling, with the hood up over her hair, so that all that was to be seen of her was her thin, pallid face. She had resorted to mascara again and the effect of it, in the shadow of the hood, was faintly gruesome. It was easy to imagine her, Peter thought, as a member of some religious cult addicted to chilling austerities, or possibly sadistic orgies. But as she came down the stairs the black habit swung open, showing healthy tanned flesh and her little bikini.

"I was just going out," she said petulantly. "What d'you want me for?"

"It will not take long," the chefe said. "I would like you and Mrs. Raven to answer a few questions. I may say you are not compelled to do so. It might be that you would wish first to consult an *advogado*. No doubt you are acquainted with one."

"Thanks, we don't want to get mixed up with any lawyers," Colonel Raven said. "The questions are quite simple. They can answer them. Come along, Harriet. Come on, Sarah. The senhor chefe wants your alibis for the time Alec was murdered, that's all there is to it. Even Sarah's capable of that, I hope."

He hobbled forward into the living room, leaving the others to follow him.

They did so, Harriet saying shakily, "You said the time when Alec was murdered, James. You did say murder?"

"Explain it to them, will you, Senhor Chefe?" Colonel Raven said. "I'm not sure I'll get it right. Someone seems to have made off with a lot of eggshells when they shouldn't have. Queer thing to have done, but it's the important clue. Listen carefully."

Once more Raposo went through his reasons for believing that Alec Methven's death was murder. Harriet and Sarah sat side by side on the sofa, Sarah, as she listened, beginning to tremble and Harriet reaching out to take her by the hand. When the brief explanation was over Harriet let out her breath in a long sigh and turned her head away to look out at the English-looking garden, as if something consoling might come from it.

"I can't believe it yet," she said. "This sort of thing doesn't happen to one. But of course I understand and I do believe it. What is it you want to ask us, Senhor Chefe?"

The chefe and Colonel Raven had both sat down. Peter preferred to remain standing. He saw that Harriet's face had become grey-white. It was less easy to tell what had happened to Sarah's, in the shadow of her hood.

"I would like you both to tell me where you were from about twelve o'clock on the day of Mr. Methven's death until the middle of that afternoon," Raposo answered. "We know from his maid that he was alive at twelve, and the medical examiner has said that he must have been dead by three o'clock at the latest. So if you will tell me where you were during that time, and whether or not you noticed anything unusual at Mr. Methven's house, any visitor arriving there, for instance, I should be very much obliged. You understand, this is informal. Later I may have to ask you to come to the policia to make an official statement and sign it, but anything you can tell me now would be helpful.''

Harriet gave a thoughtful nod. ''Yes, I see. Well, in the morning I took the car and went down into the town to do some shopping. I went to the market to buy some vegetables, then to the fish market, and I got home — oh, I suppose about ten-thirty, so you aren't interested in that, are you? It's too early. But beginning at the beginning helps one to remember. I did a few jobs about the house after that, then I started cooking and I was in the kitchen until about twelve-thirty, I think, when I went to call my husband from his study to come out and have a drink. Then —''

''A moment, please,'' Raposo interrupted. ''May I ask, did you go into the study and see him there earlier than twelve-thirty?''

''No,'' she said.

''And did anyone come into your kitchen and see you there while you were working in it?''

''Well, Miss Baird came in to ask if she

165

could have the car, as she was going swimming.''

''What time was that?''

''I really can't remember.'' She turned to the girl. ''Sarah, can you?''

''I should think it was around eleven o'clock,'' Sarah said in a low voice, ''but I can't say for sure.''

''And your kitchen, it does not face the street?'' Raposo went on. ''You could not see from the window if anyone came to Mr. Methven's house.''

''Well, no,'' Harriet said. ''That's to say . . .''

''Yes?'' the chefe prompted her.

''I couldn't see anything from the kitchen window, but I've just remembered, I went into the front garden for a few minutes to pick some flowers for this room, and I saw — but I wasn't paying attention, so I really can't tell you anything much.''

''Did you see someone arrive at the house, or leave it?''

''Yes, someone came. . . . A man. . . .'' She turned again towards the garden, as if she might be able to visualize the figure out there among the rose bushes. "I think he was short and stout and had a beard. He had a rather artistic look, I thought, and I wondered if he was someone interested in Mr. Methven's paintings and hoped he was, because he needed encouragement."

"How old was he?"

"Oh, I don't know. I'm never any good at guessing people's ages, but he was youngish — say, thirty, or something like that."

"Dark or fair?"

She gave a shake of her head. "I don't know. He had a straw hat on."

"But his beard. You noticed that. Can't you remember its colour?"

"I think it was — let me see — reddish. And he was wearing a green shirt and cotton trousers."

"Had you ever seen him before?"

"Not that I remember."

"Of course, there's a lane at the back of those houses over there," the colonel said. "If someone came up that way from the town, neither of us could have seen him, even from the garden."

"That is true," the chefe agreed. "Now, Mrs. Raven, let us go back to what you did after your husband joined you for a drink."

"We had lunch about one, then my husband went to lie down and I sat out on the patio, doing some sewing. I was still there when Miss Baird came back about half-past three. She'd had lunch at the buffet at the Victoria, and —"

"Please," Raposo interrupted once more. "I would prefer to let Miss Baird tell her own story. Thank you, Mrs. Raven. Now, Miss Baird, would you mind telling me how you spent the time between eleven o'clock, when you looked into the kitchen to ask if you could use the car, and three-thirty, when you rejoined Mrs. Raven?"

Sarah did not answer. She had withdrawn her hand from Harriet's and held both her hands tightly clasped in her lap. She was looking down at them, with her hood so far forward over her face that it was almost hidden.

The silence lengthened out, till Colonel Raven suddenly said harshly, "Sarah,

168

please answer when you're spoken to!"

"Don't talk to me like that!" she flashed back at him. "I'm not a child."

"You're behaving like one," he said.

"James, please," his wife said. "Give her time."

"What does she need it for, unless she's going to make up some lies?"

"I don't need to make up any lies," Sarah said. "I've a better alibi than either of you. I did have lunch at the Victoria buffet and they'll remember me there. I drove down there and had a swim, then had lunch, then lay around in the sun for a time — not that there was really any sun to speak of — then had another swim, then came home. I didn't notice the time I did all these things, but I think I had lunch about twelve o'clock, anyway, I know it was rather early, and if Harriet says I got home at three-thirty, then that's what I did. Then I went up to my room and got dressed and stayed there reading till we met for drinks down here later. That's all."

"Did you speak to anyone while you were down at the pool or the buffet?"

Raposo asked.

"Only to the waiter when I paid him," she answered. "But we chattered about this and that. He knows me quite well."

"Thank you. That is very clear. Now there is one more thing I would like to ask you all. I have already asked Mr. Corey and he cannot help me. But you knew the ways of Mr. Methven and his household better than he does and may be able to tell me what I want to know. The maid, Angela, tells me there was a key with a small piece of red ribbon tied to it in a china tray on the writing table in Mr. Methven's dining room. That key is missing. And Angela does not know what it was the key to, but thinks it may have been a spare key to Mr. Methven's house. And last night someone entered the house and searched it — entered as if he came in with a key, leaving no signs of having broken in — so you see, I am very interested in it and would like to know, have any of you ever seen this key? Has it ever been mentioned to you? Did you know of its existence?"

No answer came from either of the

Ravens, or from Sarah. A moment passed in which they all sat quite still, not even looking at one another. Then, almost as if it had been at a signal, they all shook their heads. It had been a moment of extraordinary tension and when it passed Harriet let out a little sigh and seemed to sink more deeply into the cushions of the sofa on which she was sitting.

"I can't remember ever noticing any key," she said. "But then one wouldn't notice a thing like that unless one's attention was drawn to it for some reason."

"No, I never noticed it either," the colonel said. "Why should I?"

"You, Miss Baird?" Raposo asked.

She shook her head without speaking.

Peter could not have felt more clearly than he did, even if they had all admitted it, that they were lying. They knew something about the key. It meant something to them.

Glancing at Raposo, he noticed a new intentness in the man's dark eyes and thought that he had come to the same conclusion. But he did not pursue the matter. Repeating that he might want them to make their statements officially and adding that meanwhile he was grateful to them for their helpfulness, he left them, returning to the house across the street.

Peter would have left with him, but Harriet checked him.

"Oh, Mr. Corey . . ." she began; then, as she paused and her husband left the room to show Raposo to the door, she went on, "Won't you stay to lunch? It'll only take me a little while to get it and you and James can have a drink while you're waiting."

"What about me?" Sarah said. "It's too late to go swimming now and I could do with a drink after being grilled like that."

"Then of course you can have one — you don't have to ask," Harriet said with the first sound of impatience that Peter had heard in her voice when she had been speaking to her goddaughter. "Won't you stay, Mr. Corey?"

James Raven, coming back into the room, heard her. All his earlier friendliness vanished.

"Oh, of course, stay," he said, in the same ironical voice that Peter had heard the evening before. "Move right in on us, if you want to. My wife will make you welcome. Even at a time like this, when we've just learnt that one of our best friends has been murdered — yes, shockingly murdered, while we sat here having lunch — she's got to have people round her. Only you'll forgive me if I go and sit by myself for a time to digest the news. I don't feel like sitting around, chatting about it. I want a little quiet. But stay — oh yes, stay. We are very hospitable."

A bright flush coloured Harriet's cheeks and a look of pain came into her eyes.

"Thank you," Peter said, "but I think I'll get back to the Victoria."

Unexpectedly Sarah came to his assistance. "I'll drive you down," she said. "Come along, the car's in the garage. I don't think I'll have that drink, Harriet, just at the moment, but I'll be back soon."

Taking Peter by the arm, she urged him out of the room.

Zipping up her black robe as she stepped out of the house, as if in a sudden attack of modesty, she put on a pair of sunglasses that she had in her pocket. A skeletal figure, bony, black, and eyeless, she turned into a kind of ghoul. Leading the way to the garage, she got into the car and backed it out into the street before she leant over to open the door for Peter to get in beside her.

"So now you've seen one of the little scenes that makes life in our household so pleasant," she said as they started down the hill. "Charming, wasn't it? So good mannered."

"It's my second of the kind," Peter said. "I ran into one of them yesterday evening."

"Well, do you understand now why I think Harriet needs me?" she asked.

"As to that," Peter said, "I'm not sure whether your being here helps her at all. A moody character, your godfather. A continuous audience may only add to the strain of putting up with him."

"He isn't my godfather," she said. "He and Harriet didn't even know each other when I was born. They haven't been married so very long, you know. Only about eight years. I think that's partly why he's so insanely jealous of her, because that's the trouble, of course, as I expect you realised. He can't bear her to be interested in anyone but him, even mildly interested, as she is in you. She is, you know. I know the signs, and so does he, and he's always terrified that sort of feeling will grow into something more and he'll lose her. If I were her, I wouldn't stand it, I'd pack up and go, but she's much too loyal to do anything like that. Jealousy's the main reason why he hates me so, you know. He can't bear it that she loves me — even me. And he hated Alec. That's what none of us has told that policeman yet, though I expect he'd be pretty interested in it, wouldn't he? I might do it sometime, if James goes on picking on me and Harriet all the time.''

''Are you trying to tell me that she and Alec were in love?'' Peter asked.

''In love, in love — in beautiful, romantic love!'' she sang out mockingly. ''Is that the only feeling a man and a woman like them can have for one another? Is that what you think? Are you as bad as James? I never said she was in love with Alec, did I? I'm only saying James hated Alec because she liked him, and all that best friend stuff is bloody hypocrisy. But I expect you think I don't know much about love. You think I'm too young. But the young can know all about it, you know, and I know it's a terrible thing. It can completely destroy you."

"Only if you want it to," Peter said, feeling helpless because he half agreed with her. "All kinds of things can destroy you if you want them to, even quite innocent-seeming things."

"Oh, you aren't taking me seriously. That's a pity. Somehow I thought you would. I thought you were a — a —" She fumbled for a word. "A perceptive sort of person. Like Alec. I could talk about anything to him. Now I suppose you're going to say I was in love with him."

"Were you?"

She brought the car to a jolting halt in front of the hotel. Sitting back with her hands still on the wheel, she stared straight before her, the sunglasses making her face inscrutable.

After a moment she said, "I've only been in love, really in love, once, and I don't mean to let it happen again."

"How old are you?" Peter asked.

Making a fist of one of her hands, she pounded with it on the steering wheel. "Don't patronise me. I'm eighteen. That's old enough to know what hell is."

"Yes, even a young child can know that. And I've been told the only way out of hell is straight through." But he was afraid he sounded horribly sententious and changed his tone. "Anyway, I expect you'll find your own way out sooner or later, so don't despair yet. Honestly, you've got plenty of time ahead of you." He began to get out of the car. "Thanks for the lift."

"I think I may tell that policeman about James's jealousy," she said sombrely. "I think he ought to know about it. And James knows how to use a gun, having been in the Army. Had you thought of that?"

"I'm sure the chefe has thought about

177

both things already," Peter said. "If I were you, I shouldn't meddle."

"You don't like me much, do you?" she said. "I thought you did yesterday, while we were having lunch, but now you don't. What have I done?"

"I'm a little afraid of you, that's all," he answered. "I'm always a little afraid of people who see themselves as the centre of the universe. They can do desperate things."

She shook her head. "You don't understand. You just don't understand. But at least you listen. That's something. Good-bye."

Peter remained where he was until she had driven away, then he went into the hotel, passing the great bowl of flowers on the marble table in the entrance hall and making his way to his own room. It took him only a moment to realise that it had been searched since he had been in it last.

CHAPTER 11

Peter went to the bar and ordered a large whisky. He felt angry and rebellious. He supposed that it was the police who had searched his room and recognised that when you were in a foreign country this was not the kind of thing about which it was wise to make a fuss. But all the same he felt furious at this invasion of his privacy and wondered if the real reason why Raposo had wanted to see him that morning had been merely to make sure that he was out of the way while the search was made.

Peter had just ordered a second whisky when Michael Searle came into the bar. He held his tall body in a stooping, slouching way, as a sulky child does, and his eyes, which were usually so friendly, had a glitter in them that made them look dangerous.

"Hallo, where have you been all the morning?" he asked, coming to Peter's side and speaking aggressively, as if he were trying to pick a quarrel with him. "I've been looking for you."

"I've been up at Alec's house," Peter said. "The police wanted to see me."

"D'you know what they did while I was swimming?" Michael said. "They searched my room. The bloody nerve of it!" He broke off to order a gin and tonic. "Then they got hold of me, told me Alec had been murdered, and questioned me for about an hour. Did I search Alec's bedroom while you were over at the Ravens'? Did I search it last night? Did I know anything about a key that's missing? Did I know where Alec's income came from? And they took me over it again and again, not a smooth character like our friend the chefe, but an ugly bastard who seemed to want to prove I could have murdered Alec while I was still in London.

I got sick of it by the end and lost my temper. But then I realised that that was just what they wanted me to do, because they thought if I did lose control I might give something away unintentionally. As if I wouldn't give it away happily if I knew anything! I want to know who murdered Alec as much as they do."

One or two people at the bar turned to listen to him curiously.

"Let's get over by the window," Peter said. "There's a little too much company here."

He led the way to one of the tables near the long window from which they could see across the bay of Funchal, past the long row of tall hotels that rose like a cliff from the water's edge. As usual, the mountains that rose beyond the town were half-hidden in mist.

Sitting down, he went on, "My room was searched too and I've been asked more or less the same questions as you. There's something disgusting about a search through one's personal belongings, but I can't see there's anything to be gained by protesting about it. I suppose it

181

was the police who did it."

"Oh yes, it was the police." Michael crossed his long legs as he sat down sprawling in his chair. "They told me so."

"Did they tell you what they were searching for?"

"I don't think they know themselves. They were simply looking for anything suspicious. I think it's because of the two times Alec's house seems to have been searched. But you know all about that, of course. In fact, you thought I'd done the searching the first time, didn't you? Probably you still do. You may even think I tried again last night. I didn't — I went to the casino for a short time and the porter here saw me come in quite early and he can tell you I didn't go out again. And I don't know a damned thing about any searching or any missing key."

"If it's any comfort to you to know it," Peter said, "the police have a theory that the two searches were made by different people. One was in a hurry and very careless, the other was very careful and tidy. And it's the careful, tidy one they think is more likely to have been the murderer.''

"So he couldn't have been me, any more than he could have been you, since we've both got our nice alibis," Michael said. "And it beats me why you think I might have been mad enough to make that first search, knowing you'd be back in a few minutes."

"Because in fact I can see you being just mad enough to risk it, though no doubt I'm quite wrong," Peter said. "Anyway, it's only a theory, as I expect Raposo would say. He seems to be very addicted to theories."

"A bloody rotten theory. I'm not a maniac. I want another drink. What about you?"

"No thanks."

"I'd like to drink all the afternoon," Michael said, turning to signal to a waiter, then relapsing into his sulky-looking sprawl. "I've been meaning to ask you, have you ever met Alec's wife?"

"Yes," Peter said.

"Do you know her well?"

"Pretty well. She illustrates my books."

"Oh, of course, you're a writer, aren't

you? Now who told me that? It must have been Alec sometime. He must have talked to me about you. I thought your name was vaguely familiar, but I couldn't place it. What's she like?"

"Clare? Well, very talented, very pretty, very good company." Peter had no desire to attempt a more informative description of her. "Have you never met her?"

"No, and Alec hardly ever spoke about her. I gathered the marriage was never happy and they pretty well hated one another by the time they broke up. He never thought of taking me to see her. It wasn't as if she was any relation of mine."

"I don't know what Alec's feelings were," Peter said, "but I don't think Clare ever hated him. You can be incompatible without hatred entering into it. As a matter of fact . . ." He broke off. He had been on the edge of telling Michael that it had been at Clare's request that he had come to see Alec, that she had been worried that he might be struggling along in poverty while she was relatively prosperous and could be helping him at least a little. But it would be just as well, he thought, not to mention that. He did not see how doing so could involve her in what had happened here, yet he had a feeling that somehow it might.

But thinking of Clare and her concern that Alec might be really poor, if he was reduced to teaching English to taxi drivers, brought Peter's thoughts back to a subject that Michael had mentioned earlier. "You said the police asked you if you knew where Alec's income came from. I suppose you told them you didn't."

"Of course I did. I've always assumed he did rather well in some job in Zaire and invested the money successfully. I've never thought about it much. It wasn't my business."

"No," Peter agreed. "Anyway, I imagine the police will ferret it out. There'll be his will, if he made one, and his bank statements, and perhaps share certificates and letters to his lawyer. I suppose he had a lawyer. D'you know anything about that? Was he here or in England?"

"I can't remember Alec ever talking

about it," Michael replied. "I've a sort of feeling he may be in Lisbon. I don't know why I think that. I know Alec used to go to Lisbon quite often and perhaps he dropped some remark about going to see his lawyer, but I can't really remember it."

"It's one of Raposo's theories that his money may have come from blackmail and that the reason for the searches, as well as the murder, may be connected with that. He's got an idea that someone may have been trying to get hold of whatever it was that Alec was holding over him."

Michael started forward in his chair.

"That's unspeakable. Damn the man's bloody theories! He didn't know Alec. It — it isn't thinkable that he'd dabble in blackmail. He was a good man." His voice was rising. "He was generous, understanding, he'd help anybody —"

"Excuse me," a voice from behind Peter interrupted, "I don't want to butt in, but I couldn't help overhearing what you were saying at the bar and I gathered you knew Methven. Alec Methven. And I wondered if there's any truth in the

186

rumour that's circulating in the hotel that he's dead. Murdered.''

Turning his head, Peter saw Frank Pelley, the man who had lain beside him on a lounging chair by the pool the morning before and tried to talk to him. Now that he was dressed in a loose yellow shirt and well-pressed white trousers, his tall, spare figure had a look of distinction. Without the disguise of his sunglasses, his eyes turned out to be an unusually pale shade of grey, almost matching his grey, curly hair.

Without waiting to be invited, he sat down at the table with Peter and Michael. He sat on the edge of his chair, hunched forward, holding his glass in both hands between his knees. They were long, bony hands that looked very strong.

"I knew him slightly, you see," he said. "I met him at the casino and somehow got talking, as one does, and he invited me up to his house once or twice. I'm terribly sorry to hear the rumour's true. It *is* true, is it? He's dead?''

"I'm afraid he is," Peter answered.

"You're friends of his, are you?" the

man said. "You knew him well?"

"I was once a friend of his," Peter said, "but I hadn't seen him for a long time." He introduced Frank Pelley and Michael to one another, adding, "Mr. Searle is Methven's nephew. He knew him far better than I did."

Frank Pelley shifted his gaze from Peter's face to Michael's.

"My sympathy," he said. "I was very shocked to hear the news."

"How did you hear it?" Michael asked with an aggressive note back in his voice.

"Oh, it's going the rounds," Pelley answered. "I think I heard it first from the waiter who brought me my breakfast. Yes, that's who it was. He was very excited about it. He said it was robbers, that the house had been looted by a gang and objects of great value stolen. I didn't believe it. I mean, I've been in Methven's house and I didn't see any objects of great value lying around. But allowing for some exaggeration, I supposed there might be some truth in it. And I'm truly sorry that there's more than I thought."

"There was no looting," Peter said.

"Even the money in Methven's wallet wasn't taken."

"And no gang?"

"I think the police regard it as a one-man job."

"How was he killed?"

"He was shot through the temple."

"By someone he knew, then? Is that what the police think?"

"It seems probable."

"That's terrible, just terrible." A slight shudder shook Pelley's lean body. "Terrible however it happened, but much worse somehow if it was someone he trusted. I liked him, you know. I was interested in him. I'm an art dealer and when we got chatting in the casino we got on to painting. He told me he painted a little and to tell you the truth, my heart sank. If there's one kind of person I've no time for, it's an amateur. But when he asked me up to his house he hardly let me even look at his pictures. And they were better than I'd expected. Not things I could do anything with, but still, they had something, a feeling, a sense of life. . . . I told him so, but he didn't seem to care.

He said he'd started much too late in life to get anywhere. As a matter of fact, he made a remark that intrigued me. He said he'd started everything too late in life to get anywhere, but he'd found out that didn't matter, he'd got what he wanted. He was a lucky man, he said. He'd had luck just when he thought he was about finished. But it's from the couple of visits I paid to his house that I know there wasn't anything of much value lying around. Some nice things — he'd had taste. But there was nothing there to attract a thief."

"Did you meet his friends the Ravens?" Peter asked.

Pelley shook his head. "No, I've met a number of people around the hotel, but I can't say I remember that name."

"Have you been here long?"

"Some weeks. I'd a nasty operation in the winter and came here to recuperate. Going back to Methven, he told me he'd been in the police in Hong Kong at one time. I was out there myself for a while, trying to pick up a little about Chinese art — my firm goes in for it — and I sometimes got the feeling I'd seen him before, so we may even have met, though I'd forgotten his face."

Peter was thinking that if Pelley could afford a fairly lengthy convalescence at the Victoria he must be doing very nicely out of his art dealing.

Michael stirred restively, finished his drink, and stood up.

"I'm going in to lunch," he said. "See you around, I expect."

He slouched off.

Pelley also stood up. "Interesting talk," he said, unaware, apparently, that he had done most of the talking. "But it's a shocking thing what happened to poor Methven. Puts me off the thought of food. I'll have another drink, I think. Will you join me?"

When Peter declined, he went back to the bar. Wondering what the man had really wanted with him, Peter finished his drink and followed Michael to the restaurant.

When he had had lunch he went to his room and lay down on the bed. It seemed to him that the day had already been going on for a long time and that the time in the morning when he had not yet known that Alec's death was murder was very long ago. He felt that he needed a rest. Was this simply what came of being middle-aged, he wondered, or would the shock of finding oneself close to a murder have a numbing, enervating effect on most people?

He was not a person who ever felt exhilarated by violence, though he realised that many did. From the adolescent viciousness of football fans to the more desperate evil of terrorists, the lust for violence was to be seen everywhere. And perhaps, after all, he was more attracted by it than he cared to admit, since he liked so much to settle down quietly with a drink in the evenings to watch the television news. For what was news but murder, rape, kidnapping, hijacking, fraud, to pick just a few standard items? A piece of good news was occasionally thrown in as a tailpiece, to be rounded off usually by the newscaster making an impromptu little joke about it and giving a tolerant smile. But if people became accustomed to the idea that there was to be nothing but good news on television, no one would trouble to watch it. Pondering vaguely on these things, Peter drifted off to sleep.

He had a dream in which Edward Otter appeared to him, dressed in the grey cotton uniform of an agente, with a rubber truncheon hanging from a broad leather belt. Even in his dream Peter had the feeling that there was something seriously wrong about this. It occurred to him that this might not be Edward Otter at all, but some other character, possibly a mink, impersonating him. For Edward Otter was not given at all to the wearing of uniforms, even one that looked as comfortably slovenly as that of an agente. He was a very pacific animal who, besides uniforms, disliked parades, demonstrations, protest placards, and mindless slogans. He was a sly creature, it was true. He liked to achieve his ends by cunning, by being just a little bit cleverer than his opponents, and when he was successful, as of course in Peter's stories he always had to be, he usually sent his defeated enemies home with generous gifts of lollies and ice cream. So what was he doing dressed up as a policeman, with a nasty-looking truncheon at his side?

The answer seemed just about to come to Peter when he woke and most of the dream faded almost immediately. He was left only with a feeling that possibly he had always been wrong about Edward Otter and that he had more of the detective in his make-up than Peter had ever realised. And if Sarah had been right that Edward represented at least a side of himself, did his dreams signify that he felt it was for him to solve the problem of Alec Methven's murder? If so, since he had hardly any access to evidence, it was completely absurd.

Shifting his position in bed, he suddenly became aware that the sky that he could see from the window was a clear, serene blue, sparkling with sunshine. There was not a cloud to be seen.

He got up and went out on to his balcony. The morning's wind had died. The palm trees below him were motionless and the sea had the satin sheen of complete calm. He decided to have a swim, hoping that he would not encounter Sarah or Michael or Frank Pelley. He was lucky in this and had the rest of the afternoon to himself. The swim had an excellent effect on his nerves, leaving him feeling pleasantly relaxed and ready to leave the whole problem of the murder in the hands of the chefe da policia judiciaria. He had a drink by the pool, staying there till the shadow of evening crept across it.

But soon after eight o'clock, when he was in his room, changing into his suit to go down to dinner, the murder once more intruded forcibly into his life with the ringing of the telephone.

He picked it up and said, "Yes?"

"Peter?"

He did not have to be told who it was.

"Clare!" he said. "When did you get here?"

"This very minute," she said. "The porter's only just dumped my luggage and left me to myself. I want to see you."

"Yes, of course. Now?"

"Say in a quarter of an hour. I

195

want to change."

"In the bar, then? But, Clare . . ."

"What?" she asked.

"I cabled you that Alec committed suicide. It isn't true. I may as well tell you at once, they think it's murder."

"That doesn't surprise me," she said. "All right, then. In a quarter of an hour in the bar."

The line went dead. Peter put his telephone down and went on with his changing.

CHAPTER 12

It took Clare only twenty minutes to arrive in the bar. She was wearing a long white pleated dress with a scattering of scarlet flowers on it and high-heeled black sandals. Her soft fair hair was looped smoothly down each side of her face, on which there was a little more make-up than usual, which did not disguise the fact that her light blue eyes, under their puckishly arched eyebrows, looked very tired.

Peter kissed her on the cheek and received a rather absent smile from her.

"You're looking well," she said. "Madeira suits you."

"In different circumstances I dare say it

would," he answered. "There's peace and luxury. What will you have to drink?"

"Since we're on Madeira, dry Madeira, please."

He ordered it for her and whisky as usual for himself, then they went to sit at one of the tables in front of the long window. She gazed out at the glittering lights on the hillside across the bay with her face curiously empty, as if she were not really seeing them.

"You meant what you said, I suppose," she said after a moment. "Alec's death was murder."

"And you said it didn't surprise you," Peter said.

"No, it doesn't really. When I read in your cable that he'd committed suicide I just couldn't believe it. He wasn't that kind of person. I don't believe he valued his life a great deal and he might easily have got himself killed in action somewhere, but the only kind of thing I could think of that might have made him kill himself was if he'd discovered he'd got some awful sort of slow disease, one of those paralytic things, for instance, that would have made him dependent on other people. But when you said it was murder, that seemed quite rational. He'd a gift for making enemies.''

"I think you're going to find that the Alec they know here is a very different person from the one you used to know,'' Peter said.

She brought her vague, unfocussed gaze round to his face. "What do you mean?''

"Well, the Alec we used to know in Hong Kong was a man of action, wasn't he? He hadn't much use for purely intellectual things. Yet here he seems to have had no other interests. His house is crammed with books. He'd a hi-fi and a mass of records. He'd taken up painting and had more ability than you'd expect. So sometime during those years in Zaire, or wherever he went after giving up being a mercenary, there seems to have been a character change.''

"I wonder if there really was,'' she said.

"D'you mean those were his real interests all along?''

"I only know of one real interest he had,'' she answered, "and that was money.

He was crazy to get hold of it somehow and that was why he went as a mercenary. The pay sounded wonderfully good compared with what he was getting as a policeman. And that was one of the reasons why I left him. I pleaded with him not to go, but he wouldn't listen, and I wasn't prepared to wait till he chose to come home again." Her voice sounded very weary. "How did it happen, Peter?"

"He was shot in the temple with a revolver," he said. "There was a not very convincing attempt to make it look like suicide, but the police saw through it fairly quickly."

"What are they like, the police here?"

"There's a man called Raposo in charge, who's pretty good, I think."

"I suppose I must let them know I've arrived and go and talk to them." She gave a sigh of unhappy resignation. "Your cable arrived yesterday morning. I decided straightaway I'd come, I'm not sure why. I don't know what I thought I could do, after all. But I was still his wife. Luckily I got a seat on a plane quite easily. Peter, I'm sorry I got you into this. If I hadn't persuaded you to come you'd never have gotten involved in this horrible business."

"You couldn't have known that," he said. He was concerned by her air of exhaustion. She seemed to be far more moved by Alec's death than he would have expected.

"No, all the same I ought to have known it was a stupid thing to get involved with Alec again," she said. "If he'd wanted it himself, he could have said so long ago. And my worrying about his living in poverty and wanting to help him, you knew at the time it wasn't real, didn't you? I was really just immensely curious about him. I'd had several letters from him over the years, all from Madeira, so it seemed as if he'd settled down at last. I started to wonder how he was living. Among other things, was he living alone? You haven't told me that. Was he?"

"Quite alone, so far as anyone knows," Peter said. "He seems to have turned into pretty much of a recluse. He'd a few friends and a nephew he seemed very attached to, Michael Searle, who's here at the moment. He and I travelled out on the same plane. And Alec gave English lessons to some local people, I think just for the interest of the thing. He can't have needed money.''

''The money,'' she said. ''Ah.'' She sipped a little of her Madeira, then leant her head back against her chair, gazing up at the ceiling. It was an ornate ceiling of white and gilded plaster and except that she had her unfocussed look and might have been staring straight through it, she might have been critically studying the moulding. ''Is it known where it came from?''

''Not so far, but they'll find out sooner or later.''

''I wonder if it was something very illegal.''

There was a touch of amusement in the way she said it which made it hard for Peter to determine how serious she was. But he was used to that in her. She often said things that she meant seriously in ways that made it sound as if she was deliberately talking nonsense.

''Is that what you'd expect?'' he asked.

''Why not?'' she said. ''If ever he'd had

the chance to get his hands on a fair amount of money, I don't think he'd have missed it, legal or illegal. He didn't take bribes in Hong Kong, but I know, if he'd ever been offered enough, he'd have taken them.''

''Well, since you practically brought the matter up yourself,'' he said, ''I'll tell you something the police are wondering about. They're curious whether or not he could have been living on blackmail.'' He told her about the two searches of Alec's house. ''So you see,'' he went on, ''they've thought of the fact that Alec may have been in possession of something that he was holding over someone, which one person, possibly Searle, wanted to get hold of so that he could go on using it himself, and which someone else, probably the murderer, wanted to get hold of to free himself of the perpetual threat.''

She looked at him once more with a directness that was unusual in her.

''I don't believe that,'' she said. ''He wasn't cruel. In a way, he was a very good-natured man, tolerant, quite generous. If you understand me, I can see him robbing a bank and making off with the proceeds and then giving away half of what he'd got, but I can't see him sitting back patiently blood-sucking and driving someone to distraction over several years."

"Searle testifies to his generosity," Peter said. "From the time his mother died, Alec looked after him, sent him to an expensive boarding school and helped to support him at Cambridge. He may even have been supporting him till now. Searle, I gather, is a not very successful actor and he may have gone right on depending on Alec."

"What's he like, this boy?"

Peter shrugged his shoulders. "A bit of an actor all the time, as most actors are, but my impression is that he cared quite sincerely for Alec. And I can guarantee he isn't the murderer, because he's got the same alibi as I have."

"Tell me, what makes the police so certain it's murder?" she said. "You haven't explained that."

Peter told her about the undigested egg and the missing eggshells.

Again she looked faintly amused, but this time as if it was she who did not know if he was to be taken seriously.

"And that's all?" she said.

"Isn't it enough?"

"It rather sounds as if our murderer is a pretty ignorant character, doesn't it, not to know a thing like that would come out in the post-mortem?"

"Or didn't expect a detective as subtle as Raposo."

"Well, I must go and talk to him, I suppose. Let's go and have dinner, then I'll see if I can find him."

"I'll come with you, shall I?"

"No, I'll manage on my own. He'll want to talk to me by myself anyway."

"It's just that you look so tired. Can't you leave it till tomorrow?"

"I'd sooner get it over. But it's true I'm tired. Flying always tires me, even when it's as easy a journey as this was. Repressed fear, perhaps. Half of me expects to go crashing into the ocean. And then there was the thought of murder, having to face it. . . . Well, let's go and eat. I may be just hungry."

She stood up and Peter stood up beside her.

They were halfway down in the lift to the restaurant before it occurred to him that she had just spoken of the murder as if she had known of it before she left London. A slip, probably. She had meant suicide and had only said murder because it was what the two of them had been talking about and because she was tired and muddled.

Clare was very quiet at dinner. She had a haunted look, as if the thought of her coming interview with the police filled her with apprehension. Peter again urged her to put it off till the next day. The police did not even know she was here, he said. They would not be expecting her. But she answered that she was sure it would be best if she went to see them immediately. She and Peter talked for a little of Edward Otter and Peter's idea of sending him to the Highlands to meet his kin there and Clare said that if he did that she would have to take a trip there herself to make sure that she got the background of streams and mountains and the wild flowers accurate. She would like doing that, she said, but she said it with a sadness that Peter found strange. Had she really cared so much for Alec?

Her sadness communicated itself to him and he found himself thinking of the time when he and she would have made the trip together and the knowledge that there was no point in even suggesting such a thing to her now made his heart ache. She might agree to go with him, which would be slightly worse than if she refused. It would only give her the opportunity to show her underlying indifference to him and she would not spare him. But that evening she looked as if she needed him, or at least someone. Perhaps there was someone else to whom she could have turned more warmly if he had happened to be there. That was something that Peter knew nothing about and did not want to know about. It had been a long time since he had tried to discover any of the secrets of her private life.

He saw her into a taxi, once more offering to go with her and being told that she thought it best to go on her own.

Only just before getting into the taxi, she said suddenly, "D'you think I'll have to look at him?"

"At Alec?" he said. "I don't know why you should, unless you want to. Searle's made an identification, I believe."

"I don't want to," she said. "I'm frightened of death."

"Aren't we all?"

"I mean, of the dead. I know it's childish, but it would scare me horribly to go near him. Who was it found him, d'you know?"

"I did."

"You? You didn't tell me that. How terrible for you." She touched his arm, searching his face curiously for a moment, as if she wondered what that discovery had done to him, then she got into the taxi and was driven away.

Going back to the lounge for the coffee that Clare had decided to do without, Peter realised that he had told her really very little about the murder, but thought that probably the chefe would tell her a great deal more. More perhaps, than she would want to be told, if her fear of the

208

dead, with their dark secrets, was as great as she had said.

He thought that this must be true when they met next morning by the pool. She had telephoned him from her room and asked him if he intended to swim and when he had said that he did, had said that she would join him later, but that first she must go to the boutique in the hotel to buy a swimming suit.

"Isn't it stupid of me, I didn't think of bringing one?" she said. "I wasn't thinking about things like swimming when I packed, but I may as well do it now I'm here. The police seem to want me to stay around for a while and it'll help to pass the time. They kept me a long time last night, questioning me about my movements and sending someone up here to get my passport to check that I couldn't have been here at the time Alec was shot. That man Raposo questioned me about you too." She gave a faint laugh. "He knew, of course, that you couldn't have done the murder yourself, but he seems to think you may know more about it than you've told him. He was interested in your reason for coming here. He seemed to think it was a strange coincidence that you should decide to renew your acquaintance with Alec at the very time when he got himself killed. I didn't tell him anything about my having asked you to come. I thought that might just lead to needless complications. He was interested enough already in our relationship. I told him it was purely professional, but I'm not sure if he believed me, though it happens to be true, doesn't it?"

"I suppose you could call it that," Peter answered.

"Well, if I'd tried to tell him the real facts, he'd never have understood them, would he?"

"I can't say for sure that I do myself," Peter said, "so he probably wouldn't."

"I'll see you presently, then," she said, and rang off.

Peter got into his swimming trunks, beach robe, and sunglasses, took an Eric Ambler with him, and went down to the pool.

The morning was fine once more, with the shining sky cloudless and the air so clear that for once the peaks of the mountains behind the town were visible. He had shed his beach robe and settled himself comfortably on one of the lounging chairs to warm up in the sun before having his first swim when he realised that the seat beside him had been taken by Frank Pelley.

"A perfect day for a trip into the mountains," he said. "Does the idea of that appeal to you at all? We could hire a car, with or without a driver, and go right across the island and down to the north coast. I've been told it's wonderful."

"I don't think I'd better fix up anything at the moment," Peter said. "A friend of mine has just arrived and may have other plans."

"Ah, and there are the police too, aren't there?" Pelley said. "I suppose they may want you still. I was forgetting about that. You haven't heard anything more about poor Methven's death since yesterday, I suppose."

"Nothing at all."

"Well, I wish I could help in some way. I've wondered if I ought to go to the police and tell them I knew him. Only slightly, of course, but I'd been to the house. If I went there I might be able to tell them if anything seemed to have been touched."

"It couldn't do any harm."

"But you don't think it would do much good either."

"You never know."

Pelley grinned, showing his teeth. "I know one thing. You think I'm butting in here where I'm not wanted. And you're probably right. My trouble is I'm always interested in people and I found Methven a very interesting chap, apart from this queer feeling I've got that I'd met him before. . . . Good Lord!"

He broke off, staring.

Clare was coming towards them, wearing a dark purple swimming suit and carrying a flowered beach robe over one arm. Her skin looked very white among the tanned sun bathers, but it had its own kind of healthy glow. She was walking slowly, looking around her, as if she had not yet seen Peter, then suddenly saw him and came faster towards him.

212

"Quick, tell me who she is," Pelley muttered hurriedly to him. "I know her — I've seen her somewhere — God, yes, that's it, Hong Kong! How could I ever have forgotten her, a woman like that . . . ? But what's her name? Introduce me, will you?"

CHAPTER 13

Pelley got quickly to his feet. Peter stood up too.

"Mrs. Methven," he said. "Mr. Pelley. Clare, Mr. Pelley thinks you've met before."

"Methven!" Pelley exclaimed. "Of course, that poor chap's wife. I'm sure you don't remember me, Mrs. Methven, I've aged a good deal since we last met, but I recognised you the moment I saw you. And Mr. Corey will tell you, I had a feeling from the first that I'd met your husband somewhere, though I couldn't place it. But now I've met you the thing's clicked and I remember him quite distinctly. I remember you both. Well,

well, what a pleasure! No, of course I don't mean that, the circumstances being what they are. A shocking thing to say. I'm most deeply sorry for what's brought us together again. I'm no good at expressing myself, but I'd like to offer you my most profound sympathy."

Clare looked at him coolly. "My husband and I had been separated for fifteen years," she said. "I came here merely to see if I could help in any way. I'm sorry I don't remember you, Mr. Pelley." She turned to Peter. "Shall we go down to the sea? I'm never very fond of swimming pools."

The way down to the sea was by a series of staircases cut into the cliff. It was a long descent, but at the bottom there were rocks and clear green waves moving gently against them and the scent of seaweed. There were far fewer people there than round the pool, which made it peaceful. At some distance from the shore there was a raft on which several figures lay prone, one or two of them rising from time to time to dive into the deep water round it.

Clare and Peter settled themselves on a

shelf of rock and Clare immediately began to tuck her hair away into a bathing cap made up of white and purple flowers, showing that she meant to waste no time in plunging into the sea.

But as she stood up, small, delicate, tiny-waisted, ready to make her way to the ladder that led down to the water, Peter remarked. "So you did know him, didn't you?"

"I did what?" she asked, pausing with most of her hair still not tucked away out of sight.

"You knew Pelley," he said. "You recognised him as soon as you saw him."

"What makes you think so?"

"Only that if he'd been a genuine stranger, you'd have been far more polite."

"Well, all right," she said, "I do remember him vaguely, but I'm not in the mood to pick up with people whom I just happen to have met years ago and of whom my only clear memory is that he was a pretty frightful bore."

"You know, I think he overdoes that," Peter said. "I don't find it really convincing."

She gave him a puzzled frown. "What does that mean exactly?"

"That I think he's chosen to present himself to us as the sort of bore who blunders in with endless tactless questions, but that that simply doesn't go together with the rest of him. He's a far too vital type. But I don't pretend to understand why he's doing it."

She thought it over, then shook her head, finishing tucking her hair away into her cap.

"I think he was always like that. Very disappointing, actually. One had hopes of him when one first met him. He was very good-looking, as you can imagine. His hair was black then, and with those pale grey eyes it was pretty striking, and he had lots of that vitality you're talking about. But when you tried to talk to him there was simply nothing there. There's nothing particularly extraordinary about that. Sometimes it works the other way about. People who strike you at first as utterly commonplace turn out to be fascinating."

"Oh, that's all quite true, of course, but

there's another odd thing about him," Peter said. "Why does he pretend not to be sure if he'd ever met Alec before?"

"Perhaps because he really isn't."

"When Alec had a name like Methven? It isn't exactly a common name. Knowing someone called that, I don't think I'd forget it, even if I couldn't remember a thing about the man himself."

She frowned again, looking at him curiously. "What are you trying to prove, Peter?"

"I'm not sure," he said, "except that there was more of a connection between him and Alec than he wants us to realise."

"Then why doesn't he simply keep away from us? That would be the best thing for him to do."

"Because for some reason the murder means something important to him and we're the most available source of information. He's intensely curious about it."

"I expect it's just morbid interest," she said. "That's common enough, isn't it?"

Turning away from him, she started across the rocks towards the ladder, moving cautiously on her small, bare feet, which plainly felt painfully tender. Peter got up and followed her.

The sea, which was almost as still as the pool above, though a good deal cooler, felt strangely exhilarating compared with it. It was deep and clear, with sunlight penetrating its surface so that for a long way down, until the gleam melted into shadows, it was a pale, transparent green. Clare was making for the raft. Swimming in her wake, Peter thought what an extraordinary thing it was that he and she should be here together in a place like this, which once would have meant to him a happiness beyond belief, yet now meant so little.

Or was that just his good old defence mechanism at work? He had been hurt by her too often to lay himself open to it again, now of all times, when he had so much else on his mind. If he was careful about it, he could be contented in her company, and at his age, wasn't that enough?

Not that he was as old as all that. It was only that in this kind of environment, where one was surrounded by bevies of the almost naked young, supple and unself-consciously beautiful, one began to worry about that putting on of weight and so on, which had not seemed important before, and to wonder whether after all one should be strong-willed before it was too late and cut down on one's whisky. . . .

Something slim and brown, striped with little bands of yellow, flashed through the air, cleaved the water cleanly near Peter, and surfaced again a few yards beyond him. Sarah Baird shook her drenched hair back from her face and came swimming towards him with a few easy strokes.

On the raft, on to which Clare was just climbing, Michael Searle stood with his hands on his hips, looking at Sarah.

"That was fine," he called out to her. "Now watch me and tell me what I do wrong."

He balanced on his toes for a moment on the edge of the raft, then dived, but not nearly as well as the girl.

"Well?" he said, coming up an instant later, brushing water from his eyes. But then he recognised Peter. "Hallo," he said, "I'm sorry, I didn't see who you were. Don't you usually stick to the pool?"

"He's generally too lazy to come all the way down," Sarah said, laughing. The sound of it made Peter realise that it was the first time that he had heard her laugh. Also her eyes had a brightness in them that he had not seen before. Her long hair floated around her like seaweed. "Isn't it a heavenly day? It hasn't been so marvellous for weeks."

Peter would not have believed that she could look so alive and so nearly beautiful.

Michael was just behind her. Suddenly putting his hands on her shoulders, he thrust her downwards. A moment later she bobbed up again, spluttering and lunging at him, covering his face with one hand and trying to push him under the water. He slid away from her, while both of them crowed with laughter. Peter got out of the way of the horseplay and climbed up on to the raft, sitting down beside Clare.

"Michael," he called out, "you'd better

come up here and meet your aunt."

Michael looked up in surprise, then came to the raft. There was no one else on it just then but Peter and Clare. Michael held on to the edge of it, looking up at her. There was some astonishment on his face, as if she was not at all as he had imagined her.

"You're Clare?" he said.

"And you're Michael," she responded.

"This is a funny way to meet after all these years."

"It's as good a way as any. If it's a good thing to have met at all."

He gave her the smile that made him look so charming. "Oh, it's a good thing, I'm sure. You haven't anything against me, have you?"

"It's a question of what you've got against me."

"I suppose you hardly knew of my existence."

"Hardly," she agreed. "And what you know of me won't have been specially pleasant, as it was told to you."

"Actually Alec told me almost nothing about you. You were rather a banned subject. But I'd have expected something, well, more formidable."

"It's difficult to look formidable in a swimming suit on a raft in mid-ocean."

They laughed together. To Peter's relief, friendly relations had been established. It would not have helped matters just then if there had been tension between them. But Michael, of course, had his actor's need to make a good first impression, while Clare had always been skilled at concealing her feelings. The friendliness might never go any deeper than the surface. But for the time being at least it would help to keep things comfortable.

Sarah scrambled up on to the raft.

"Nobody's introduced us," she said to Clare, "but you're Mrs. Methven, aren't you, and I'm Sarah Baird. Alec was a great friend of mine. I live in the house just opposite his. That's to say, I'm staying there at present with the Ravens. Mrs. Raven's my godmother. They were great friends to Alec too, in fact, I think almost his only close friends. He was a very withdrawn sort of person, wasn't he? But he and Harriet — that's my godmother — liked each other very much. James — that's Colonel Raven, but he isn't my godfather, he and Harriet hadn't even met when I was born — James and Alec just put up with each other because they were neighbours. But James is an awfully difficult person. If he can't push you around, he's got no use for you, and no one could push Alec around."

But the girl's thrust for attention had failed. Clare was much more interested in Michael than she was in Sarah. She said vaguely, "I see," and looked back at Michael, who had let go of the edge of the raft and was lazily treading water. "How long is it since you last saw Alec?" she asked him.

Sarah answered before he had a chance to do so. "It's two years since he was here. I was here too then. We're old friends. And we're going to take a picnic lunch with us and drive up into the mountains, as we used to then, and go walking. It's wonderful up there, you know, above the trees, with the peaks all bare except for the giant heathers and the clouds white and soft-looking below you, blotting out everything except the other peaks across great chasms, jutting up out of the clouds like islands. You ought to try it too."

"I avoid walking whenever possible," Clare replied. She looked back at Michael. "So it's a whole two years, is it?"

"Well, actually I've met him once or twice in Lisbon," Michael said, "but only for the odd day or so."

"Why in Lisbon, why not here?" she asked.

Again he had no chance to answer, because Sarah took it into her head at that moment to dive back into the sea. The dive was a flash of movement, beautiful to watch. Bobbing up just beside Michael, she flung an arm round his neck and repeated her manoeuvre of trying to duck him. Breaking away from her, he went swimming off at great speed, with Sarah chasing him. Their very youthful laughter rang out happily as they grappled with one another.

"What a pestilential child," Clare observed.

Peter had been thinking that although

the girl had been chattering too much and as always had been determined to be the centre of attention, there had been something very refreshing about seeing her so happy instead of glowering, and for once immensely enjoying the company of a youthful male. He wondered if Michael had been wily, inducing her to go swimming with him, which she did so much better than he did that she must have felt far more self-confident than usual.

"What did she mean by that crack about how much Alec and her godmother liked one another?" Clare asked. "Did she think it would make me jealous?"

"She's capable of it," Peter admitted. "I don't know if she's right about it."

"These people, the Ravens — that policeman talked about them. Who are they?"

"Just what Sarah told you, neighbours of Alec's."

"Could I see them, do you think?"

"I should think it could be arranged."

"Then will you do that?" She stood up. "I'm going back now. I don't want to

226

get scorched.''

She went down the steps of the raft into the water and swam off in a leisurely way towards the rocks of the Victoria.

Peter presently telephoned the Ravens from his room and was answered by Harriet, and when he told her that Mrs. Methven had arrived and would like to meet her and her husband, was at once invited to bring her to tea that afternoon. He and Clare had lunch together at the buffet on the terrace below the swimming pool and saw Frank Pelley there, but perhaps because Clare had been so short with him earlier, he appeared not to see them. After lunch they went to their rooms, agreeing to meet in the entrance hall at four o'clock.

Peter settled himself on his balcony with his book, but found himself distracted by that question of Clare's that Michael Searle had not answered. Why, if he and Alec had met from time to time in Lisbon, had Michael never come the small distance further to Madeira? And also, what had he been doing in Lisbon? Did they make, say, Western films in Portugal, as they did in Spain, and was that what had taken him there? Was it a case of Alec's going to see Michael, because he had happened to be working in Lisbon, rather than Michael's coming to see Alec? But then Peter remembered Michael's telling him that Alec had a lawyer in Lisbon and wondered suddenly if his trips to Portugal were somehow connected with his rather mysterious income. And did Michael know a great deal more about that than he made out?

But perhaps the two of them had met in Lisbon simply because they liked it there. It was important, at a time like this, to remember that people often acted for simple, irrational, human reasons.

Punctually at four, he went down to the entrance hall and found Clare waiting for him. She was wearing very well-cut jeans, a white silk shirt and her silver ring with the big white topaz in it. Her skin had reddened a little from the sun in the morning, but she looked cool and elegant.

As they got into one of the taxis that seemed always to be waiting at the gates, Peter asked, "Is there any special reason why you want to see the Ravens?"

"Not really," Clare answered as the taxi started, "except that I'm trying to pick up the threads of Alec's existence after we separated. Just curiosity, I suppose."

"Is that really all?"

"Oh, it's a way of filling in time too. I'm stuck here for I don't know how long. I may as well see if they're people I can talk to."

"You aren't trying a little detecting of your own on the quiet?"

"What, me?" She laughed. "Would it shock you if I said it doesn't matter to me very much who killed Alec? The reason it happened intrigues me rather, but don't sentimentalise our relationship, Peter, simply because Alec's dead. We weren't happy together and we were glad to separate. Murder's horrible and it's terrible to think it happened to him; all the same, what I'd like best now is to go home. I wish I'd never come. But of course I can't leave, so why shouldn't I go and see the Ravens? But we'll call it off if it worries you."

"It doesn't worry me in the least," he

answered. "It's just that I like to know where I am."

"What are they like?"

"You'll see. I don't think they're your type. And if the colonel's extremely rude to you, don't blame me."

"People are very seldom rude to me," she said. "If they are, I generally blame myself." The taxi stopped at the gate of the pale blue house. "Come along," she added, "let's see if I can tame him."

CHAPTER 14

There was no immediate need to tame the colonel, because, as Harriet told them, he was lying down. His rest, apparently, was an important part of his day, which he did not interrupt merely to greet visitors. She took Clare and Peter out to the patio, telling them how glad she was to meet Clare, then hesitating, with a slight flush on her cheeks, as if she feared that this had not been at all the right thing to say, then going on to say it again, though somewhat differently.

"You'll forgive me if I say I was always curious about you," she said. "Sometimes I had the feeling that Alec was almost afraid of you, but I'm sure that can't have been right, except that I believe he was afraid of all human relationships, except perhaps with the very young. That's why he was so good to Sarah. And that was wonderful, because it was just what she needed at the time. She'd been through a horrible experience and I'm afraid my husband wasn't as understanding as he might have been, though of course he was always kind in his way. But Alec was different. He really helped her.''

She had sat down with Clare and Peter, then stood up, saying something about getting the tea, then sat down again, but on the edge of her chair, ready to take off once more in a moment. Clare's cool poise had brought out all the shyness in Harriet. But she was looking very attractive in a sleeveless dark red dress and with an unusual glitter in her eyes, as if Clare's presence was causing her some kind of inner excitement.

"I can imagine he would," Clare said with detachment.

Harriet nodded eagerly. She could not take her eyes off Clare. Had she always thought of Clare as a kind of enemy,

Peter wondered, the person responsible for making Alec turn away from human relationships and in so doing making him inaccessible to her? Now, faced with Clare herself, she had found that this view of her had suddenly become unreal?

Harriet struck Peter as one of the people who find it painful and unnatural to dislike anyone. It would only be in the abstract that she would be able to remember to feel any bitterness, even if she thought herself injured. And had she in fact been injured at all by Alec? Had she ever been in love with him, and if she had, was there anything to show that he had not responded?

"I'd like you to meet Sarah," she went on. "Of course, she hasn't really been herself since Alec's death, it's shocked her so terribly. It's been like living through her father's death all over again, as I told Mr. Corey. But I'm sure she'll tell you how much he did for her."

"I think I met her this morning in the sea," Clare said. "She didn't seem to be suffering much from shock."

"She was with Michael Searle," Peter

explained. "They seem to have made friends again. She told us they were taking a picnic lunch into the mountains and going walking."

"She did?" A delighted smile lit up Harriet's face. "She's really doing that? That's wonderful. That's a great step forward. They used to be such friends when he was here before, so when they met again I hoped something like this might happen, but she seemed to want to have nothing to do with him, any more than with any other boys near her own age. I'm afraid I'd rather given up hope of his being any help. But they're really spending the day together, are they? Oh, that is good news. Now I'll get the tea. I shan't be a moment."

Springing up from her chair, she hurried into the house.

Clare looked at Peter with raised eyebrows and he responded with a faint shrug of his shoulders; then they sat there without saying anything until Harriet reappeared, carrying a tray with a cloth on it of fine Madeira embroidery, a silver teapot, cups and saucers, and a plate of biscuits. Her mood had altered while she had been in the kitchen. She looked more composed and sure of herself.

"I expect, like most people, you think I worry too much about Sarah, Mrs. Methven," she said. "But the truth is, we've had a very difficult time with her and sometimes I've despaired. You see, she's the nearest thing I've got to a daughter and she means a great deal to me. I've told Mr. Corey some of her story, though not all of it." She turned to Peter. "I told you, didn't I, she had an unhappy love affair and the man ditched her just after her father died, so she took an overdose of sleeping pills. Well, that's true, as far as it goes. But I left out the fact that she got pregnant a little while before her father's death and the man persuaded her to have an abortion, hinting that he'd leave her if she didn't. But if she did, so she understood, they'd get married and have children later when they could afford it. So she went ahead with it — she'd taken me into her confidence and I helped her arrange it — and then the man left her all the same. So it was then she took the overdose." She was pouring out the tea. "She was very young, only sixteen, and I've told you this, I suppose, to explain why I feel so responsible for her, because the disaster was partly my fault, wasn't it? I believe now it would have been better for her to go ahead and have her baby, even if she had to bring it up alone, rather than do something that went so completely against her instincts. I'd also like you to understand her if sometimes she seems a bit strange."

"It's a horrible story," Clare said. "Poor girl. What happened to the man?"

"Oh, he went off with someone else." One of her anxious looks appeared on Harriet's face. "You won't let her know I've told you this, will you? She'd be very angry with me." She handed round the plate of biscuits, and again looking at Peter, inquired, "Do you think Michael will be here long?"

"I shouldn't think so," he answered. "He'll go back to England as soon as the police let him go."

"That's a pity, of course," she said, "but perhaps, now the ice is broken, things will be better. We're probably going back to England ourselves fairly soon."

"For a visit, you mean?" Peter said.

"No, permanently. We haven't really made up our minds, but we've been talking about it for some time. With the pound so low, Madeira's really become an extremely expensive place to live. An army pension doesn't go very far. We think we might be a good deal better off in England."

"Where would you go?" Peter asked.

"I'd like to go to Dorset. I grew up there. It's a beautiful county, isn't it? But James says if we go at all it had better be to London. He's got his club there and still a few old friends, and of course, if you're a sick man, it isn't too wise to bury yourself in the country. So I expect it will be London. Is that where you live, Mr. Corey?"

"Yes," he said.

"Then perhaps I can ask your advice about where to live. I used to know it quite well, but it's changed so in recent times, everyone tells me. I really shouldn't know where to start."

"I don't expect you'll find me much help, but I'll do what I can," he said.

"That's very kind. You must remember to leave your address with us before you go. Do you live in London too, Mrs. Methven?"

Clare smiled and nodded. "Yes." She deliberately made the word sound ambiguous, Peter thought, to leave the other woman uncertain as to whether or not she and Peter lived together.

"Of course I know your illustrations to Mr. Corey's books," Harriet hurried on. "They're so delightful. I wish I were creative in some way, but I've no talents at all. I do so envy the people who have. It was different when I worked, but now I feel I'm of no account whatever."

"I don't think anyone should feel like that," Clare said. "And it almost certainly isn't true. Look at what you've done for Sarah. If she pulls through successfully, it'll have been your doing, won't it? I feel I've never done anything that amounts to much for anyone but myself. Tell me, d'you think Alec was happy in his last years here? I'm sure you're the kind of

238

person who'd have known, if anyone would.''

Harriet looked uncertain, as if such a direct question was a little too much for her.

"I don't think I know a great deal about happiness," she said. "It's a thing that comes and goes, isn't it? More often than not you look back and say, 'I was happy then,' but you don't realise it at the time. But I'd say he was fairly contented anyway.''

"You don't know of any special worries he had?''

"I never noticed anything to suggest it.'' Harriet wrinkled her forehead in a puzzled frown. "You aren't thinking it may have been suicide after all, are you, because I think the police are quite sure it was murder.''

"No, but even murder doesn't usually come completely out of the blue," Clare said. "There are things leading up to it, like threats, for instance. Did he never speak as if he was afraid of someone, or seem to be taking odd precautions of any kind, or doing anything at all strange?''

Harriet gave a slow shake of her head and repeated, "I never noticed anything."

"I really shouldn't be bothering you with these questions," Clare went on, "but I know so little about what happened to him during all these years we've been apart and I can't help wondering about them. And if the murder really came out of the blue, then it seems to me it must have been connected with a theft of some sort. That's what the police think too, I believe, from what they told me yesterday evening. But they can't get any information about anything valuable he had."

"They've asked us about that too, of course," Harriet said, "but we couldn't tell them anything. If he had anything like that, he must have kept it hidden."

"So only someone who knew him pretty intimately would have known of its existence."

From the doorway, Colonel Raven said, "I happened to overhear that, Mrs. Methven, and I've another suggestion to offer. Someone out of Alec's past, who was with him when he acquired this thing, whatever it was, would have known he had it." He came limping into the room, shook Clare's hand, gave Peter a friendly nod, as if today he had nothing against him, then lowered himself into a chair and asked if there was any tea left. As his wife went out to fetch another cup, he went on, "That's what I'm inclined to believe. I think someone who used to know Alec long ago came to Madeira on a holiday, met him by chance and remembered this ancient treasure of his. Then he came to visit him as a friend, killed him, looked for the treasure and couldn't find it, so he came back a night later and that time presumably did find it. If he didn't I'm sure the police would have discovered it by now, to go by the way they've been taking the place apart. Not that they know what they're looking for, of course, which doesn't make things easier for them. But what d'you think of that as a possibility, Mrs. Methven?"

For a moment Clare said nothing. It suddenly struck Peter that her posture had become oddly rigid. Then she seemed to force herself to relax.

"It could be, I suppose," she said.

The colonel, accepting the cup of tea that his wife had brought him, smiled at Clare benignly. "I hope I'm not distressing you by talking about it."

"I want to talk about it," she said. "I want to understand it."

"I thought that would be how you'd feel. But I suppose you can't think of anyone who fits my theory, can you? Anyone you used to know in Hong Kong, for instance."

"I — don't think so," she said uncertainly. Peter would have liked to know why she said nothing about Frank Pelley but did not interrupt. "It could be anyone he'd met later during those years in Zaire, if that's where he stayed. In fact, if there's anything in your idea, it probably was."

"True, that's the likeliest thing. He must have mixed with some pretty wild characters while he was there. Now let's talk about more cheerful things. How do you like Madeira?"

Clare replied that she had hardly thought about the question so far and he replied that that was only natural, then went on to advise her on the trips that she should take about the island before she left. It was Peter's impression that the old man had taken a decided fancy to her and was doing what he could to charm her. He said that if she was interested in the island embroidery, his wife would be able to show her the best shops, and Clare, whose acquisitive instincts were easily roused, responded a little to that, but on the whole she was subdued, more than she had been before he had come into the room. Soon she said that she and Peter must leave. Harriet said that she would have offered to drive them to the Victoria, but that Sarah had taken the car that morning, and of course had not returned, but she offered to call a taxi.

To Peter's surprise, knowing as he did that Clare did not care for walking, she said that she thought a walk would be pleasant and the two of them set off down the hill, after having been pressed by the colonel to come again as soon as they liked and to let the Ravens know if there was any way in which they could help them.

The evening was fresh and cool, with a faint breeze stirring the blue fronds of the jacarandas along the street.

"You see, he wasn't at all rude to me," Clare said. "I told you he wouldn't be. He wasn't rude to you either."

"I think that was because I was in the company of a woman who didn't happen to be his wife," Peter said. "He's got a very jealous streak."

"I should think with reason."

It surprised him. "How d'you make that out?"

"Didn't you notice the way she looked at you?"

"I can't say I did."

"Oh dear, you were never very observant about that kind of thing, were you? I've pointed it out to you before."

"And I think it was generally your imagination."

"You think I'm jealous, like the colonel?" She laughed.

Peter laughed too, rather wryly. "The opposite, I should think. You work so hard at trying to find another woman for me."

"Well, it would be good for you. Are you really not at all interested in that woman?"

"I might be, if she hadn't other attachments."

"Do you think they're really going back to England, or is that just a daydream of hers?"

"I think they might really be going. I know they're worried by the expense of living here."

"Isn't there something a little odd about their deciding to go now?"

He glanced at her as she walked beside him. Her tone had been casual and she was looking about her at the unfamiliar flowers in the gardens.

"What's on your mind, Clare?" he asked.

"I just thought myself it's a little odd," she said. "Alec gets murdered and they immediately decide to pack up and go back to England."

"I can't see any possible connection."

"No? You may be right, but I just don't care for coincidences at a time like this. That woman's very frightened of

245

something, isn't she? She's not far off panic. Perhaps they've some good reason for bolting.''

Peter remembered his own earlier impression that something had frightened Harriet badly, but dismissed it once more as being merely the result of her shyness.

''It might be that Alec's death was somehow a deciding factor in getting them to make up their minds to go,'' he said. ''I've a feeling they're really pretty lonely here and losing their closest friend may have made them feel there was nothing to stay on for.''

''Were they really such close friends?''

He looked at her again and this time found her eyes on his face, intently curious.

''I believe you're wondering if one of them's the murderer,'' he said. ''Oh, come!''

''I'm wondering about everybody,'' she answered. ''I'd wonder about you if you hadn't been on that plane — as you'd wonder about me, if I hadn't been safely tucked away in London.''

''Do we really trust each other as little

as that?'' he asked.

"Oh, I don't think you've ever trusted me much, except to produce your illustrations for Edward Otter,'' she said. "You rely on me for that. But one day the creature's going to drop dead, and what then?''

"What makes you say that, of all things?''

"You'll grow out of him sometime, that's all. His days are numbered.''

Peter found the remark extraordinarily upsetting. He did not reply. Not that he took her seriously. But what she had said roused an uneasiness that was already at the back of his mind. It had in fact been there from the start. He had never entirely believed in Edward Otter's chances of survival. Every time that he finished a book he had a feeling that he would never have an idea for another. So far a new idea had always arrived in time, but would that go on indefinitely? Wasn't it time to start thinking of new ways of earning the comfortable living to which he had become accustomed? And apart from that, he was beginning to find it difficult to believe in Edward Otter's continuing victories over the mink. In a confrontation, the mink would inevitably win. The violent were usually successful.

"Don't look so worried, Peter," Clare said, slipping an arm through his. "I didn't mean it. Edward Otter has many happy and successful years ahead of him."

Again Peter did not reply. Clare looked as if she was aware that she had started something and was wishing that she hadn't. They finished the rest of the walk to the hotel almost in silence.

Both went to their rooms when they got there, arranging to meet presently in the bar. Peter started to change into his grey suit. But suddenly he had an overwhelming desire for a drink immediately, a drink by himself, with no need to discuss murder with anyone, or to ask himself troublesome questions about the future. Just a peaceful and comfortable drink all alone.

He had not had nearly enough time alone during the last few days. Normally he had so much of it that he had no reason to think about how much he needed it, though he knew that the constant pressure of other people round him always made him tired and irritable. That was how he was feeling now. And there was plenty of time to slip down to the bar straightaway and have the quiet drink he craved before changing and joining Clare there later.

Abandoning his suit where he had just dropped it on the bed, he went out to the lift and down to the bar, only to discover when he got there that Clare had had the same idea as he had. She had not yet changed for the evening and was sitting on a stool at the bar, nursing a drink in both hands and gazing thoughtfully before her.

But she was not alone. Frank Pelley was with her, his cheek against her hair and his arm round her shoulders.

CHAPTER 15

Peter's first impulse was to turn away quickly before they saw him and go back to his room. But curiosity stopped him. Crossing the room to the table by the window which he was almost beginning to think of as his, he sat down with his back to the bar and gave his order of whisky and soda to the waiter.

He wondered what they would do when they saw him. Slip quietly away, hoping that he had not seen them? Come and talk to him, making a joke of the fact that they had pretended to be casual acquaintances when it was obvious that they knew each other very well? And would Frank Pelley drop his pose of being a harmless, chattering bore when in fact, as anyone could tell who had seen him just now with Clare, he was a vigorous man, powerful and dominating?

For a little while none of these things happened and Peter's thoughts began to probe other questions, mainly concerned with the implications of what he had seen. But presently he heard Clare's light footsteps behind him and she sank into a chair beside him.

"Well?" she said.

He glanced round and saw that Frank Pelley was stalking out of the bar towards the lift.

"Well?" Peter echoed.

"So you saw us," she said, "and now you think you know everything."

"Is there a lot to know?" he asked.

"Oh, you infuriate me," she said. "Why do you never get angry?"

"Anger's very tiring," he said.

"Tiring!" she exploded. "Is that all you've got to say? Frank and I deceive you about how well we know one another and you just call it tiring!"

"D'you want me to make some kind of

big protest about it? I don't see I've any right to, except in so far as you've both tried to make use of me. I rather resent that. But your life's your own. After all, it always has been.''

''So as long as I turn out your bloody illustrations for you, you don't care what I do.''

It amused Peter that she was working hard to put him on the defensive.

''I've been taught not to care, haven't I?'' he said. ''I learnt the lesson well.''

''Don't you even want to know about Frank and me?''

''I think I know most of it. There's just one thing I'm curious about. Has it been going on ever since Hong Kong days, or only started up again recently?''

''It's been on and off ever since we met. Frank isn't a person who could ever settle down in one place, with one woman, yet I've never been able to get him out of my system. But what did you mean about our making use of you?''

''Clare, am I a fool?''

''Sometimes I think so, but let's not go into that.''

"Shall I tell you what I think happened, then?"

She leant back in her chair, watching him with a new look of wariness. He seemed not to be behaving quite as she had expected.

Realising that she was not going to reply, he went on, "To go back to the beginning —"

"The beginning isn't important," she interrupted.

"But I think it is. The beginning was in Hong Kong, when you and Pelley first met. And it was because of that that Alec went off to the Congo. I thought your marriage broke down because of me, but it was really because of Pelley, wasn't it? I don't know what things were like for you before he arrived on the scene, perhaps not so good, but anyway, that put an end to everything. By the way, what was he doing in Hong Kong? He says he was an art dealer, trying to learn something about Chinese art, but that doesn't seem likely."

"We'll come back to that later. Let's go on now."

"All right. Alec went away and from

that day to this you never saw him again and you knew nothing about how he was living, though you had an occasional letter from him. You knew when he settled in Madeira, but you knew nothing about what he was living on. He told you he was teaching English to waiters and taxi drivers, so you never thought he could be prosperous. I think it may have amused Alec to give you that impression. Then Pelley, with whom you'd had this on and off sort of relationship you've talked about, came here to recuperate after an operation and he met Alec. Of course all his talk about feeling he'd met him before but not being able to remember him was all nonsense. They recognized each other at once and Alec invited him up to his house."

"Tolerant of him, wasn't it, if you're right that Frank wrecked our marriage?"

"Shall I tell you what I think about that?" Peter said. "I've been trying to piece together what I knew of Alec and what I've heard about him since I got here and to arrive at what may be the truth about him. He was a person who simply didn't care about other people. That can happen to someone who's had a very unhappy childhood, as Alec had. The springs of human feeling seem to get dried up at the source. He never became capable of love or hate or even much in the way of ordinary affection. When Alec left you it wasn't in a rage, or because his heart was broken, but simply because it seemed to him the best way out of an uncomfortable situation. He may also have thought it was what you wanted and he may have been quite glad to please you, but I don't think there was much passion about it."

"Oh, you're right, absolutely right!" she exclaimed. "And how *could* one love a man like that?"

"I should think it must have been difficult. He was a type that ought not to marry, as I think he realised later. They're wiser if they become devoted to a collection of dogs or cats, or take up bird-watching, or something like that."

"What Alec was devoted to was money," she said. "I've told you that."

"Yes, but only so that he could lead a certain kind of life," Peter replied. "The real passion of his life was education, the thing he'd utterly missed in his childhood. But he'd also an adventurous streak in him, and he began by thinking that ranging from one kind of activity to another would sooner or later bring him the money he needed to live as he wanted to live. And in the end it did. We don't know how, but it's obvious that at some time after he went to Zaire he made a lucky strike and got away with some kind of minor fortune. So he began to do what he'd wanted to do all along. He chose a quiet, comfortable spot where no one would bother him and he began to educate himself. He read and read and he studied music and he took up painting. And he taught English to the men who couldn't afford to pay him much because he'd a great sympathy with anyone who wanted to learn. And he was friendly with his neighbours and quite well liked by them, but never became really intimate with them."

"Don't you think the Raven woman was intimate with him?" Clare asked.

"I'd be surprised if she was, if he was

the kind of man I think he was."

"But she wanted to be," she said.

"That's possible."

"And her husband thought it was rather more than possible."

"You may be right, but I think the first real intimacy of Alec's life was with his nephew and that came about because, when his sister died, he discovered Michael was going to have the same kind of childhood as he'd had himself, and that was more than he could tolerate. So he took the boy over and spent as much as he could afford on giving him the kind of education he'd never had himself and tried to steer him into becoming a scientist or something of that sort. But there Michael disappointed him. He insisted on becoming an actor. And I'm not sure if he ever gave Alec the kind of affection he wanted from him. Perhaps Alec didn't know how to evoke affection. But he used to go to Lisbon sometimes to meet Michael, when Michael didn't seem to think it worth his while to come the little extra distance to Madeira, so I think the stronger feeling must have been on Alec's side. Then he discovered someone else who was young and unhappy and so once more he put himself out to do all he could for her — Sarah.''

"This is all very interesting and I dare say most of it's right," Clare said, "but what has it go to do with Frank and me trying to make use of you, which you say you resent? You haven't explained that."

"I think it's time for another drink," Peter said. He turned and beckoned to a waiter. "Yes, I have got rather far away from that," he agreed when he had given his order, "though to me it all seems to hang together. Because it was the obvious fact that Alec was living here in moderate affluence that got Pelley interested in him. I suppose they met by chance, recognized each other, and Alec invited him up to his house; Pelley realised at once that those years in Zaire had paid off and he wanted to know how. Was there anything in it for him? Or have I got him wrong? Is he not that kind of person?"

Clare looked absently out of the window, as if she had some difficulty in deciding what to say. Lights were beginning to show on the distant hillside and there was a tinge of dusk in the sky. It turned it to a soft shade of violet. When the waiter brought their drinks she picked up hers and transferred her gaze to its depths.

"You know what you're asking me," she said. "You're asking if I actually conspired with Frank to rob Alec of whatever he's got. Is that what you really think of me?"

Peter shrugged his shoulders. "You did persuade me to come here. You did persuade me to get in touch with Alec. Wasn't that because you knew he'd never agree to see you, but you thought that in the right mood he might tell me quite a lot about himself? And you and Pelley have certainly been in touch recently. On my first morning here he was looking out for me. He said he recognised me from the photograph on the Edward Otter jackets, but I believe in fact he knew I was coming and got the porter or someone to point me out to him. And you knew that Alec had been murdered before I told you that. You were still supposed to think it was suicide when you arrived here, but you let the word murder slip out. At the time I thought you were simply confused, but now I think Pelley had been in touch with you. He'd telephoned you, hadn't he?"

Again she took time to reply, then at last she nodded.

"Yes, the morning after I got your cable. And I'm not sure why I came — Frank warned me not to — except that I was anxious . . ." She let the sentence fade.

"Anxious that Pelley had committed the murder." Peter ended it for her. "When Raven started talking about someone out of Alec's past, perhaps from Hong Kong, having committed the murder, I saw you go rigid. Because murder would have been rather more than you could stomach."

"I'm glad you realise that much about me." She looked up at him suddenly, as if she had just decided to make something clear about herself. "But it isn't what I was going to say. The truth is, I was anxious that Frank might cheat me and I wanted him to realise that I wouldn't stand for that. I've always made that clear to him. Whatever relationship he has with other people, he's got to be honest with me. And I think he has been. It isn't that I specially need money, as I think he does at the moment, or he wouldn't have troubled himself with a small fish like Alec, but just that I've got to know where I stand with him. If he's found Alec's secret treasure, then I want to know about it. He can keep it, but I won't be deceived."

"Do you think he *has* found it? Do you think he was one of the people who searched Alec's house?"

"That's another way of asking if I think he committed the murder. Because the police think it was the murderer who came back and searched the house, don't they?"

"That's only guesswork. Clare, now that you've told me so much about him, tell me a little more. What, if anything, does he do for a living? He isn't an art dealer, is he?"

"He's been one, in his time. He was a very good salesman of high-quality fakes. And he's been, and always will be, a gifted con man. He can sell rich old ladies anything. And now and then he's gone in for forgery, and he's done a bit of drug smuggling on the side. That's what he was doing when I first met him in Hong Kong and he seemed to know at once that it would be safe to talk to me about it."

"You draw the line at murder, but you don't mind drugs. Isn't that conniving at slow murder, with madness thrown in?"

She finished her drink. She looked so delicate, so innocent, and too calmly intelligent to have become involved in the things that she had been talking about.

"I think I'll have dinner in my room," she said, standing up. "All this talking has been a bit much for me. I don't feel like facing the restaurant."

"You haven't answered my question," Peter said.

"If I tried to, you wouldn't understand me," she answered. "You're a funny mixture of shrewdness and naïveté, as well as being terribly honest. That's a limitation. You could never understand how exciting it is to love a really bad man. I've learnt far more from him than from anyone else I've ever known. But he mustn't be crooked with me, that's part of

262

our understanding. And now that you know far more about me than you did half an hour ago, I expect that'll put an end to our relationship, and that will be a very good thing for you. Good night, dear Peter. In my way, I'm very fond of you, but I doubt if you'll ever want to have much more to do with me."

She touched him lightly on the shoulder, then turned and walked away across the room to the lift.

Watching her go, Peter accepted that this was the end of something. For a moment he felt a shocking sense of loss, then after it a rather pleasant sense of release, though it was irritating to realise that that was precisely how Clare had intended him to feel. She had deliberately painted herself in the blackest of colours in order to set him free of her. While she had been doing that, she had of course been setting herself free of him — and of Edward Otter, too.

She had said, only a short while ago, that his days were numbered. So possibly she had been aiming even then at bringing the present situation about. If Peter had not happened to see her with Pelley, and so given her the opening that she wanted, she would have created another herself. They would have drifted apart long ago if it had not been for Edward Otter, and obviously that would have been best for them both. That blameless animal had a good deal to answer for.

Peter knew that he could always find another illustrator, if he wanted one. His publisher would arrange that for him. But it would never be the same, even if the new illustrator was as able as Clare and capable of imitating her style impeccably, and even if Peter's readers, most of whom were under the age of ten, never noticed the difference. No, Edward Otter was doomed. And time too. There was release in that as well, just as there had been when Clare walked away from him.

He had a third drink before he went upstairs and changed and came down again to dinner. He did not see Frank Pelley in the restaurant, and thought that probably he was having dinner with Clare in her room. Michael Searle was nowhere to be seen either. Peter had a large plate of hors d'oeuvres, some fish that he could not name, which no doubt belonged in the seas around the island, a fillet steak, and some fresh fruit. He felt as hungry as he would have if he had just been on a walk of twenty miles. Not the way that one ought to feel, he thought, when one has just broken off the great love affair of one's life.

But really, if the woman preferred a drug-smuggler to him, there was nothing more to be said about it. He would start a new life when he got home to London. He would change as many habits as possible, and among others he would take serious steps to bring his weight down, cut down on his whisky, be careful about his diet, lengthen his regular walks, and generally put up some resistance to the pressure of middle age.

But not tonight. A good meal, a bottle of wine, and then a long sleep was what he needed.

He succeeded in sleeping very deeply and later than he usually did. It was the telephone that woke him. Reaching for it, still only half-awake, he thought that it must be Clare who was calling him, but it was Raposo's voice that he heard.

"Mr. Corey? I am in Mr. Methven's house. I should be obliged if you would come here immediately."

"Immediately?" Peter said. "I'm awfully sorry, but I'm still in bed. I'm not dressed. I haven't had breakfast."

"Then please come as soon as you can. It is urgent, I assure you. It is necessary that you should dress, I understand that, but perhaps for once you could do without your breakfast."

"What's the trouble?" Peter asked. "What's happened?"

"I will show you when you get here."

"*Show* me . . . ?" Peter was fully awake by now. "Has there been another search?"

"That seems probable."

"Or have you found what this character's been searching for?"

"No, not that. But I prefer not to talk about it on the telephone. It goes through the switchboard. Please come as quickly as you can."

Raposo rang off.

Peter put his telephone down, left it for a moment, picked it up again, asked for room service and ordered breakfast. Then he got up, showered and dressed. By the time that he was ready his breakfast tray had arrived and he drank a cup of coffee, but left the rest and went down in the lift and out to one of the waiting taxis.

He was scared by now, because there had been something in Raposo's voice that he had not heard before and he was wishing that he had waited to eat a buttered roll, because he knew that shock always hits hardest on an empty stomach. What the shock would turn out to be he had no idea, but he felt certain that it would be something very unpleasant.

It was very unpleasant indeed. An agente opened Alec's door to him and ushered him straight into the living room. Raposo was there, directing the operations of a man who was taking photographs of the body of Michael Searle, which lay sprawled on the floor in the middle of the room, with his head a mass of dried blood.

"Yes, it is strange," Raposo said calmly

as Peter stood there speechless. "He knew too much, that is plain. And it is interesting that he has the missing key in his pocket, the one with the red ribbon attached to it."

CHAPTER 16

Peter felt a throbbing in his head. He wondered if he was going to faint. He had taken Alec's death far more calmly. But then Alec himself had looked calm and reconciled to his end. There had been no sign of terror about him and very little horror in the sight of his body. Michael Searle's end had been far more violent. Both his hands were reaching out as if he had been trying to grasp something in his last moments and after Peter's first glance at the shattered head he could not go on looking at it. He wanted to go straight out to the patio and be sick.

But Raposo did not move.

"He was shot from in front with a

much larger gun than the one used on Mr. Methven," he said. "I think he flung out his hands to try to grasp his assailant. It is plain he saw him and knew who he was, unlike Mr. Methven, who had no suspicion that he was about to die."

"Why did you bring me up here?" Peter asked, trying to speak normally and conceal how badly he was shaken. "Am I supposed to have had something to do with it?"

"I think you knew more of Mr. Searle than anyone else here," Raposo replied. "I wanted to ask you if he said anything to you at any time which led you to think he knew more about Mr. Methven's death than he admitted."

Peter shook his head. "I knew very little about him. I met him for the first time on the plane and I didn't even know then that he was connected with Mr. Methven."

"And he said nothing to you about his uncle's murder?"

"Oh, we talked about it, but he didn't seem to know any more about it than I did."

"Yet it seems probable that he knew too much for his own good and was killed because of it."

"You think that was the motive for killing him?"

"I can think of only one other and that is that he let himself into the house when someone else was searching it again and was shot to prevent him from identifying the person."

"You still think that Methven had something valuable that various people have been trying to find?"

"Yes, indeed, we are sure of it."

"But wouldn't you have found it yourselves if there'd been anything here?"

"Not if someone else had found it before us. And we did find its hiding place, though it was empty."

He moved towards a bookcase and took down two thick, leatherbound volumes of Doughty's *Arabia Deserta*. Opening one of them, he showed Peter that the centre of the book had been hollowed out, leaving only an oblong cavity.

"And the other volume is the same," he said, flicking it open briefly, showing the same mutilation, then replacing both books on the shelf. "There are no fingerprints on them, not even Mr. Methven's own. The searcher wore gloves and carefully polished the books when he was finished with them."

"How long ago did you find these?" Peter asked, in better control of himself now.

"The day before yesterday," the chefe answered, "the morning after we found the house had been searched. Unfortunately we did not take the first search you told us about as seriously as we should have. If we had and if we had watched the house to see if Mr. Searle came back, we should have caught the man who did come and who had committed the murder. But we thought Mr. Searle's hurried search while you were out of the house could not have been for anything important, or he would not have risked making it then, and that whatever it was, he had probably found it and removed it, though we found nothing of interest in his room, any more than in your own. It was only when we saw the signs of a methodical search that we made a careful search ourselves and found these two volumes. Found them empty, because we were too late and to have kept a round-the-clock watch on the house after it would have been like locking the stable door after the horse has been stolen." He paused. "We are much to blame."

"Don't you think it may have been Searle who made that second search?" Peter said. "After all, it seems to have been he who took the key. He'd have known that it was a spare key to the house, so that looks as if he meant to come back. I suppose it *is* a key to this house?"

Raposo nodded. "Yes, and I agree with you it looks as if he must have taken it to be able to come back and search at his leisure, and the fact that the two searches seemed to be different in character, which I thought important, may merely have been because the second time he could go about it slowly and carefully. But if that was what happened and he had found the thing he wanted, why did he come back to the house last night? Was there something more to be found, or was the key that we found on him planted on him by someone else who had taken it earlier and come back and found whatever was in those books?"

"So you think Methven's murderer may have taken it straight after the murder?"

"Then or later."

"It couldn't have been later, unless it was taken by Searle. Neither of the Ravens went into the dining room while I was in the house."

"We have only your word for that, Mr. Corey," the chefe said. "And we have only your word for it that you did not take the key yourself."

A strange mixture of rage and panic seized on Peter. Like most honest people, he felt utterly bewildered when he was not believed. The practised liar, when his veracity is challenged, is generally ready with a counterattack. But Peter felt helpless and defenceless. When it came to the point, he could see no reason why he should be believed. This man knew almost nothing about him. He would have to trust to his intuition and if this was telling him that Peter was not reliable, then that was just too bad. There was nothing to be done about it. A show of righteous indignation would not help matters.

Speaking quietly, Peter said, "If you can't think of any reason why Searle should have come here last night if he'd already found what he wanted, why should anyone else have come back? I mean, if he'd already searched successfully."

"Of course to meet Mr. Searle by appointment. If something Mr. Searle had found in this house had somehow told him who the murderer was and he tried to put pressure on him, perhaps a meeting might have been arranged here, where they could expect not to be interrupted."

"Would Searle have been such a fool as to meet a man who he knew had already committed one murder here alone in an empty house?"

"Oh, Mr. Corey, people continually do the most foolish things. Some are so full of foolish fears of nothing that they hardly dare to go out of their homes, while some feel themselves so invulnerable that they take the most insane risks."

"No, admit it," Peter said, "you've no explanation of why someone who'd found what was in those books should come back to the house. Doesn't it begin to look very much as if the searching had nothing to do with the murder?"

Raposo gave him one of his long, sad looks, then after a few words with the photographer, who had finished his work and was ready to leave, walked out on to the patio. Peter followed him. They both sat down on the cane chairs there. A light breeze stirred the banana leaves at the bottom of the garden so that the tattered fringes made a slight swishing sound.

"I believe you're a writer of children's stories, Mr. Corey," Raposo said.

"Yes," Peter answered, "though they're really thrillers of a sort, written for the very young."

"Ah, thrillers," Raposo said, as if that explained something. "Now let me ask you something more. In your conversations with Mr. Searle, did he ever mention meeting his uncle in Lisbon?"

"Yes, he did," Peter said.

"Did he say why they met there?"

"He said something about his uncle having a lawyer there, but it didn't sound as if it was anything very important."

"I think it *was* important. I find it interesting that after those visits to Lisbon, Mr. Searle always went on to Amsterdam."

"How do you know that?"

"From his passport. He met Mr. Methven in Lisbon about twice a year, then went to Amsterdam, then back to England. What does Amsterdam mean to you, Mr. Corey?"

If Peter had answered honestly, he would have said that the main thing that it meant to him was the publisher who took all his works for translation into Dutch. Holland was a very good market for him. But he doubted if that was the answer Raposo wanted.

After a pause for consideration, he said, "Isn't it about the biggest diamond market there is?"

Raposo nodded his head, as if to encourage a promising pupil.

"And do you know that Zaire is the biggest producer of industrial diamonds in the world?'' he asked.

"I didn't know that," Peter said. "Oh, I see. You think Methven had a cache of industrial diamonds hidden in those books and that's what someone's been looking for."

"It is just a theory," Raposo said in the apologetic tone he always used when he spoke of his theorizing. "If your friend did not remain a mercenary for long, but took work in one of the diamond mines, then one day had the opportunity to make off with a consignment of diamonds, he could have been living on those ever since. It would not be difficult, if the chance arose, to carry away on one's person enough diamonds to keep one in comfort for a lifetime. And I should add that the cheques that Mr. Methven regularly paid into his bank here in Funchal all came from Holland."

"It sounds possible," Peter said. "But why did he only sell them in driblets? Why didn't he get rid of them all together, instead of keeping them here, where there'd always be the risk of their being stolen?"

"I think it was very wise of him," Raposo said. "With inflation what it is, their value increased greatly with the passing of time. If he'd sold them all when he first arrived from Zaire, he would only have got a fraction of what he got in the end."

Peter studied him thoughtfully. "You really believe this, don't you?"

"It is a theory."

"It's rather convincing. But why the complication of meeting Searle in Lisbon? Why didn't he go to Amsterdam himself?"

"Because sooner or later someone would have become curious about his connections in Holland. I myself might have begun to take an interest in them. We like to understand the comings and goings of our foreign residents. But to go to Lisbon frequently from Madeira is nothing. And Mr. Searle was not a conspicuous person, and if the British authorities should have started asking questions about him, which was unlikely, I am sure he had some cover story ready, perhaps a girl he visited there, or some such thing."

Peter nodded. "Yes, I see. By the way, you haven't told me how you found his body. What brought you here this morning?"

"It was the woman Angela. She came here to fetch an apron she had left behind. She had no key to the house, of course, but she thought the police might be here and would let her in. There was no one here, but she saw the body of Mr. Searle through the window. Now tell me, Mr. Corey — it is only a formality, but I must ask it — where did you spend the night from about nine o'clock until I telephoned you in your room this morning?"

"You want my alibi," Peter said. "I haven't got one. I went to my room after I'd had dinner, went to bed, and slept soundly until your call woke me. But I can't produce any witness to say I'm telling the truth. What time was Searle killed?"

"The doctor will tell us more about that later, but his guess at present is about midnight."

"And where did the gun he was killed

with come from?"

"I have another theory about that," Raposo said hesitantly. "I think it may have been taken from the drawer where we found Mr. Methven's other gun. After all, if a man has one gun, why should he not have two or three?"

"You mean it was taken by the murderer when he killed Methven? You think he'd already decided that he was going to need it, that he was going to kill Searle?"

"I have not thought that out yet, but yes, it might be so. Now please tell me, Mr. Corey, did you see Mr. Searle any time yesterday?"

"Yes, in the sea around eleven in the morning. He was with Miss Baird. They said they were going to drive up into the mountains to do some walking. If it's of any interest to you, it's my impression that he'd fallen for Miss Baird, though I don't know how seriously. Certainly he was attracted and I thought she was too. May I ask, do the Ravens know about his death?"

"Yes, I saw them after telephoning you,

while I was waiting for you to arrive. They had nothing much to tell me."

"Nothing more about a man with a red beard?"

Raposo gave the smile that he kept for the promising pupil.

"So you do not believe in him either. We have asked the other people who live in this street, but no one saw him. However, as Colonel Raven reminded us, there is a lane up from the town behind these gardens and if someone came up that way, he would not have been seen. But not by Mrs. Raven either."

"As a matter of fact, I thought she invented the man in a great hurry when she realised her husband had no alibi for the time of Methven's murder," Peter said. "I think she seriously suspected him of having done the murder out of jealousy on her account."

"I agree with you. . . . Ah, forgive me." Raposo rose suddenly to his feet as several men, two carrying a stretcher, came into the room behind them. "The ambulance has come. I must go now. Thank you for your help, Mr. Corey."

"Have you finished with me?" Peter asked. "Can I go?"

"Yes, yes. You will be at the Victoria if I should need you?"

Peter said that this was probable, avoiding completely committing himself, and going back into the living room and round the group of men who were standing around Michael Searle's body, quietly left the house. He crossed the road to the blue house opposite, let himself in at the gate, and rang the doorbell.

Harriet Raven opened the door. She was in jeans and a shirt, but today there were tearstains on her face. Her eyelids were red and swollen, her face was pale. Peter wondered what had made her weep. He could not believe that Michael Searle meant so much to her that she would shed many tears for him. She would feel shock, of course, and pity, and might have wept for him a little, as some people do at the mere thought of death. But she had been a nurse and was unlikely to have had the habit of weeping over every one of her patients who died.

She did not try to conceal the fact that

she had been crying. Brushing the back of her hand across her eyes, she said, "I'm sorry, this is stupid of me. For some reason I just broke down this morning after that man Raposo left. Everything seemed to be too much to stand. I'm just making coffee. You'll have some, won't you?"

She led Peter into the drab little living room, then disappeared to the kitchen.

Her husband was sitting in one of the armchairs. He began to raise himself laboriously to greet Peter, but when Peter told him quickly not to trouble, he dropped back thankfully into the chair. Gesturing to one for Peter, he said, "I was rather expecting we'd see you. The chefe's been putting you through it, I suppose."

"We had a rather long talk, yes," Peter said, sitting down. "He told me he'd been talking to you. But I came over because I wanted to ask you a question. If it's inconvenient now, I can come some other time."

"Time, time!" the colonel exclaimed. "It means nothing to me. I get up, I have breakfast, I read the newspaper, I have a drink, I eat, I sleep. . . . No time's more inconvenient than any other. What's your question?"

"There's a man staying at the Victoria called Pelley," Peter said. "He knew Alec years ago in Hong Kong and he says he visited him here a few times. I wondered if you happened to have met him. You suggested yourself to Mrs. Methven that the murderer might be someone out of Alec's past."

"Pelley?" the colonel said, frowning in concentration, then he shook his head. "The name doesn't mean anything to me. What's he like?"

"Age about fifty," Peter said. "Tall, thin, a good deal of curly grey hair, tends to wear dark glasses —"

"Wait, wait!" the colonel interrupted. "Yes, I've seen him. But only across the road, going in through Alec's gate. That would be about a week ago. Is he mixed up in this thing?"

"He may be, but that's only a wild guess. You can't remember if Alec ever talked about him?"

"I'm sure he didn't. No, wait a moment. That day before he died, when I had drinks with him, he did say something about having met an old friend. And then . . . Yes, it's coming back to me. My memory's shocking nowadays, that's just old age, but things come back if I don't worry too much about them. Alec said something about having met this old friend and then he gave a rather peculiar laugh and said that the word friend could mean as much or as little as you wanted it to. I didn't pay much attention at the time. He often said things like that that didn't mean much to me. But I think I see what you're getting at. You think it may have been this man — what did you say his name was, Pelley? — who made off with Alec's diamonds."

"So Raposo's told you his theory about the diamonds," Peter said.

"Yes, and I don't believe a word of it."

"Why not? I find it rather convincing."

"Well, I suppose it's just possible. . . . Harriet!" The colonel suddenly raised his voice and shouted towards the kitchen. "Harriet, do you believe in those diamonds of Alec's?"

There was no answer for a moment, then Harriet came in, carrying a tray with cups and a coffeepot on it. There was a confused, defensive look about her, as if she had already had too many questions thrown at her and could not remember clearly what she had said in answer to them.

"Diamonds, diamonds!" her husband said impatiently. "What the chefe was talking about this morning."

She put the tray down on a table and asked Peter if he would like cream and sugar. He answered that he would prefer his coffee black and without sugar. She poured it out and brought it to him. From the expression on her face she might have been concentrating intensely on how to carry a cup without spilling anything from it, and on nothing else.

"I suppose he was right," she said at last as she turned back to the tray to pour out coffee for herself and her husband. "I mean, a man like that wouldn't say a thing of that sort unless he'd some grounds for it. Then again, perhaps he was only guessing. Those journeys of Michael's to Amsterdam aren't much to go on. I really haven't any ideas about it."

"Did Raposo tell you about the copies of *Arabia Deserta* that had been hollowed out to hide something in?" Peter asked.

"No, he said nothing about that," the colonel said. "This wasn't just talk? You saw it, did you?"

Peter nodded.

"Extraordinary!" the colonel exclaimed. "So Alec was a thief. Because that's what it comes to, doesn't it? He wouldn't have been so secretive about it if he'd come by those diamonds in a legitimate way. And he wouldn't have kept them at home, he'd have kept them in the bank. That man you were talking about, the grey-haired fellow Alec used to know in Hong Kong — he's the one who took the diamonds, he must be. I don't say he murdered Alec, I don't know anything about that, but he must have come here because he actually knew what Alec had hidden away."

Harriet suddenly started talking fast, as if she had had enough of death and diamonds. "Is your coffee as you like it,

Mr. Corey? I'm afraid I've made it rather strong. I'm in a bit of a state this morning and don't know quite what I'm doing.''

The coffee was very strong, but that happened to be what Peter needed.

''It's just right,'' he said.

''I expect Sarah did the best thing,'' she went on hurriedly, as if she did not want to give her husband a chance to go on talking. ''After the chefe left, she went off swimming. This new thing that's happened is perfectly terrible for her, of course. She and Michael had just begun to make friends again and it's the first time she's even looked at a young man since her breakdown. I felt so happy about it. She seemed so happy herself when she came in after that trip they did into the mountains, just like she used to be two years ago. Happy and sort of excited, you know, as if she'd fallen in love. That may be stupidly romantic of me, but she did seem so wonderfully alive. I couldn't help wondering what had happened between them.''

''Romantic!'' Colonel Raven said scornfully. ''The chefe comes here, tells us the boy's been killed, and what does she do? She doesn't say a word. She just puts on her swimming togs, gets into the car, and drives off to the Victoria. She doesn't shed a tear. She's ice cold. If that's how she behaves when she's just started to fall in love, heaven protect any man she really sets her heart on."

"You know she never cries," his wife said. "I've often thought it would do her good if she could. I cry at the least thing. I've never been able to control it. All the same, I could see from her face what her feelings were and I could tell she couldn't have borne sitting around here, doing nothing."

For once the colonel did not retort, but allowed her to have the last word on Sarah.

Peter stood up. "I mustn't keep you any longer. Thank you for the coffee, Mrs Raven. It was a great help."

"This man Pelley," the colonel said, looking at him, "have you spoken about him to the chefe?"

"As a matter of fact, I haven't," Peter answered.

"Why not?"

"I'm not sure. I didn't think of it. Perhaps I should have."

"Yes, I'd do it, if I were you. Or I can do it myself. It can't do any harm."

Except, of course, Peter thought, to Pelley, whether or not he happened to be involved in theft and murder.

But Peter did not say this. Setting off down the hill, he considered the real question that he had wanted answered when he went to the Ravens, and which he had not asked. It was not the kind of question that it was possible to ask, and it had had nothing to do with Frank Pelley. He had wanted to know simply how the Ravens were taking the news of the murder of Michael Searle. For right from the start there had been something secretive about them. He could not help feeling that they knew more than they admitted.

And he had found that Colonel Raven was his normal self, in one of his more amiable moods. And Mrs. Raven had wept, either for Michael Searle, or else for some other reason that she was anxiously keeping to herself. And Sarah had gone swimming.

CHAPTER 17

The person in whom Peter was most interested just then was Harriet. He wished that he could see her by herself and talk to her at some length. But he saw no chance of this. If the chance arose, which was unlikely, she herself, he thought, would do her best to avoid it. For concealment did not come naturally to her and she would be afraid of letting the truth be dragged out of her too easily. The truth, or what she thought was the truth. She might be mistaken about it. But at least it would be interesting to discover what she believed she knew and the real cause of her tears.

The morning was another grey one with

low clouds hanging over the town and a cool wind blowing that sent them scudding across the sky, with only an occasional shaft of sunshine spilling through between them, and when Peter had a glimpse of the sea through a rift in the tall bank of hotels along the cliff tops, he saw that there were whitecaps on the grey water. If Sarah had gone swimming, he thought, it would be in the pool, not in the sea, where she and Michael had been playing together like young children yesterday.

He did not feel tempted to swim himself, but he wanted to talk to her. Arriving at the Victoria, he did not trouble to go to his room to change into his swimming trunks, but went straight to the lift, took it down to the level of the pool, and strolled out towards it.

He did not find Sarah there, but he found Clare. She was lying on one of the lounging chairs, well wrapped up in her robe, reading. When Peter stood still beside her, she did not look up for a moment, then she said, "Oh, it's you," and laid her book down. It was a tattered-looking travel book about the island of Madeira, which she must have found in the hotel library.

"Whom were you expecting?" he asked.

"No one in particular. Sit down." She waved at the chair beside her. "Where have you been?"

"I've been having another dose of questioning by the police," he told her, sitting down. "Where's Pelley?"

"Why?"

"I rather want to talk to him."

"I'm afraid you're too late. He left Funchal on the early plane this morning."

"Did he, indeed! That's interesting."

"Why?" she asked again.

"Because he's ducked out just in time to avoid being questioned about our second murder."

"Our *second* . . . ?" She paused, giving him a sharp, questioning look. "What do you mean?"

He told her about his summons by the chefe that morning, of the death of Michael Searle, of the hollowed-out copies of *Arabia Deserta,* and of Raposo's theory that they had recently contained diamonds. She listened without interrupting, but she looked away from him as if she did not want him to have the chance of watching any changes in her expression. When he stopped she did not speak at once.

Then she said, "You think Frank did it?"

"I didn't say that," Peter replied. "I wanted to talk to him about those diamonds that may or may not exist."

"Do you think he took them?"

"After the things you told me about him yesterday, it doesn't seem improbable."

"I suppose you told the police all those things," she said.

"As a matter of fact, I didn't."

"Why not?"

"Do you really have to ask me that? Weren't we talking in confidence?"

"So that still means something to you." She gave a sigh and looked him in the face once more. "That's what I told Frank, Peter. I said I could trust you completely. But he wouldn't believe me. That's why he left this morning. He said once the police started investigating him, he was bound to have trouble, so he was getting out while he still could."

"You told him what you'd told me about him, then," Peter said.

"Yes, and he was very angry with me. But you're wrong about him, you know. If he'd found out anything about those diamonds, or whatever they are, we wouldn't have wanted you to come out here to see if you could get Alec's confidence, would we? And I can tell you for certain Frank didn't kill the Searle boy, because he spent the whole night with me. We had dinner together in my room and he stayed on until it was time to leave to catch his plane."

"I rather thought you'd say that."

"Do you mean you don't believe me?"

He lay back on the long chair, folding his hands under his head and gazing up at the clouds that chased each other across the lowering sky.

"It doesn't much matter," he said.

"Peter, I'm telling you the truth," she said with unusual urgency. "Frank isn't a murderer."

"But you were half-afraid he was when

you first got here, weren't you? That first evening you were so drained and exhausted; I thought it was strange you should seem to feel so much for Alec, but it wasn't Alec you were really worried about, was it? It was Pelley.''

"Oh yes, I had my doubts of him," she admitted. "But now I *know* he had nothing to do with either murder, because he did spend the night with me. And if the police get around to questioning me about him, that's what I shall tell them.''

"I'm sure you will.''

Rolling over on to her side, supporting herself on an elbow, she peered into his face. "You still don't believe me, do you?''

"Oh, for God's sake, let's stop this!" Peter said. "There's something I haven't told you. A spare key to Alec's house was found on Searle's body. Alec's maid said he used to keep it in a tray on his writing table. It had a piece of red ribbon attached to it. So it looks as if Searle took it during the short time he was alone in the house while I went over to the Ravens' after finding Alec, and used it the following night to let himself into the house to search for the diamonds, which he found and removed. But if that's so, why did he go back last night? The chances are he was killed because he knew who the murderer was, but I can't believe he'd make an arrangement to meet that person in an empty house in the middle of the night. So I think he must have gone back for some other reason we haven't thought of yet. And there's always the possibility that he never took the key at all, but had it planted on him after he was dead, which means it was taken immediately after Alec's death by someone who intended to come back later to search for the diamonds.''

"But what could that have to do with Frank?'' Clare asked.

"I don't know. I'm just trying to feel out what it means. Perhaps it had nothing to do with him.''

"It hadn't. Even if he'd ever seen the key, how could he possibly know what door it opened?''

"He might just have made a lucky guess.''

"You know you don't believe that. No, Searle might have known what that key was and taken it, and so possibly might the Ravens, but Frank simply couldn't have."

Really Peter agreed with her. Whatever uncertainty there had been in his mind before he started talking, what he had said had cleared up a certain amount of the confusion. Pelley had not removed the key, had not come back to search the house, had not removed whatever had been concealed inside the mutilated volumes of *Arabia Deserta,* and probably had not murdered Michael Searle.

He sat up. "Have you seen Sarah this morning?" he asked.

Clare shook her head.

He looked at the few people who were in the pool at the moment, braving the chill of the morning, but Sarah was not one of them, nor could he see her among the recumbent bodies on the chairs around the pool.

"I was told she'd come here," he said. "Perhaps she's gone down to the sea."

"It'd be rough for swimming

this morning.''

''Still, I think I'll go and look for her.'' He stood up. ''And don't worry about your Frank. I shan't say anything about him to the police. Whatever criminal activities he's been involved in in his time, I doubt if he was pursuing them on Madeira.''

She looked up at him with a sudden brilliant smile. ''You're very good to me, Peter.''

He felt as if there must still be something important to say to her before he turned away, but he could not think what it was, and walking off to the steps that led down to the sea, he came to the conclusion that he had only been trying to find words in which to say good-bye to her, and that this was a futile thing to do. Of course they would see each other again. For the present they were held together by Edward Otter, as a child can hold its parents together in an unhappy marriage. But luckily, when the time for separation came, there would be no heartbreaking problems of custody to be settled. The wise, gentle, pacific animal, who had given them both so much, could be quietly destroyed and buried, and even if there were some regrets, no tears need be shed. And meanwhile the drama of any formal farewell to Clare was to be avoided.

Peter went on down the steps, hearing the rhythmic, pounding sound of the waves breaking over the rocks at the foot of the cliff growing louder as he approached the bottom.

He found Sarah, in her black beach robe, crouched on a rock only a little way above the spray flung up by the breaking waves. There was no one else on the rocks. She had her hood up and her knees drawn up to her chin, with her arms clasped round them. She heard him coming and looked towards him. Her sunglasses, unnecessary today in the shadow of her hood, made what looked like deep holes into her head. She watched him coming until he was almost beside her, then looked out to sea again.

"Don't talk about Michael," she said. "I've had all I can stand."

Peter sat down beside her. "What are

you doing here?" he asked. "You can't swim today."

"Isn't it obvious I came to be alone?"

"D'you mind so much, then? Had you really begun to care for him?"

"I don't care at all. Not at all. D'you understand?"

"You don't care for many people, do you?" he said. "Yet a number of them have been quite good to you — Mrs. Raven, Alec, even Colonel Raven, who may not exactly love you, but who's given you a home for quite a while. And Michael was very attracted by you. Doesn't that mean anything?"

"If you've come here to lecture me," she said, "I'm going. And Michael wasn't attracted by me, he was attracted by my money. I should have thought anyone could see that. I'm not the sort of person people fall in love with at first sight, as he pretended he had."

"But that's a thing that can happen to anyone at any time."

She shook her head stubbornly. "Not to me. I don't even want it to. What I want is to go away somewhere by myself and live quite alone. If I were religious, I might go into a convent, but I don't believe in anything. I've tried to, but it doesn't work."

"Won't you stay with the Ravens when they go back to England?"

"They won't go. They'll talk about it, but they won't really do it."

"And you don't want to stay here any longer?"

"No. Sooner or later I've got to stand on my own feet, haven't I? James is quite right. And it might as well be now."

"What about Mrs. Raven's needing you? You were very sure of that a little while ago."

"I was just kidding myself. She doesn't want me any more than anyone else does."

"You're very full of self-pity this morning."

She gave a disconcerting little laugh. "I'm not. I'm just facing facts. Isn't that a good thing to do? People always say it is." She stood up. "I'm going home now. If the police are still around, I'll drive up into the mountains. I won't be pestered by them any more. I'm tired of you pestering me too. I just want to be left alone."

"Just a minute," Peter said. "When you were in the mountains with Michael yesterday, did he talk at all about Alec's death? Did you ever have the feeling that he knew something about it?"

She twitched at her hood, arranging it around her face. In the enveloping black robe she looked as if after all she might have entered some austere religious order.

"I can't think of anything he said," she answered, "but he must have known something, mustn't he? Wasn't that why he was killed? And I shouldn't be surprised if he was meaning to make use of his knowledge somehow. He wasn't a very nice person, you know."

"But his death seems to have shaken you very deeply. Much more than Alec's, yet you were fond of Alec, weren't you?"

Her voice suddenly went up into something near a scream. "Leave me alone! Why d'you keep asking me all these questions? I've had all I can stand. I need peace. That's what the doctors said. They said I had to live quietly and not be bothered."

"I'm sorry,' Peter said. He stood up beside her. "It's just that you saw more of Michael yesterday than anyone else and I thought he might have dropped some hint about the key, for instance, that they found on his body, or about the diamonds that are missing, if that's what they were. Think about it. Didn't he say anything?"

"What key? What diamonds?"

"You remember about the key to Alec's house. . . . Oh, my God, no!" Peter stopped abruptly, staring at her, but hardly seeing the slim black figure standing beside him. "The key — what a fool I've been!" He grasped her arm. "You're going home now? You've got the car? Then take me with you. I've got to talk to that man Raposo."

From the set of her mouth he thought for a moment that she was going to refuse to take him. Then she turned away without speaking and started to climb the steps. Peter followed her. She did not turn to look back at him, or speak. She did not speak or look at him either when they reached the car, which was parked in front of the hotel, but got into it, leant across to unlock the door beside the passenger's seat, then waited with an air of indifference while Peter got in beside her. She seemed to have no curiosity about what he had said. She did not ask him why he wanted to speak to Raposo.

That suited Peter, in whose brain a number of new thoughts were going round and round and who wanted a little time to sort them out. As the car went up the hill under the soft blue tossing plumes of the jacarandas, a sense of horror grew in him, while his thoughts, as he tried to follow them, only led him deeper and deeper into a tangle. He was not really ready to speak to Raposo and yet he saw that there was an urgency about it, because Raposo might see what Peter had seen and yet not see quite enough.

He sat back in the car, finding that he was breathing more deeply than usual, as if he was afraid of what was ahead of him, as indeed he was. In the kind of life that he had lived, he had very seldom had to take any major responsibility. Except in small matters, he had hardly ever been compelled to assert himself. Such affairs as life and death to a great extent had passed him by. But now, as he saw it, he had no choice. He must insist on making himself heard.

As it turned out, there was no difficulty about that, it was only a question of how far he ought to go at once. When the car stopped at the pale blue house he saw Raposo on the pavement, standing beside a police car into which an agente was assisting Colonel Raven. The attitude of the agente was considerate enough and yet there was not quite the look about him of someone simply helping an arthritic old man to settle himself comfortably. His face was grim, his hand, on the old man's arm, not very gentle. In the doorway Harriet Raven stood quite still, her face grey and her hands hanging loosely at her sides in an attitude of complete defeat.

Raposo looked round as Peter and Sarah approached him.

"Ah, you have come back," he said. "As you see, it is as I thought from the start. I am taking Colonel Raven down to the policia to charge him with two murders and with the theft of a quantity of industrial diamonds. We searched the house this morning and found them in his bedroom in a biscuit tin, hardly concealed, he was so sure of himself. It was that missing key that told me the truth."

"So you understand about the key," Peter said.

"I think so. The key was not a spare key of Mr. Methven's house, that is the crux of the matter. Why, after all, should he keep a spare key of his own house on his writing table? The truth is that that key was the key of Colonel Raven's house. As neighbours sometimes do, each had a spare key of the other's house, in case of one of them accidentally locking himself out. The red ribbon was to distinguish it, so that it should not be confused with others belonging to Mr. Methven and he kept it where it was easily available, in case it should be needed by Colonel or Mrs. Raven. But at the same time, of course, Colonel Raven had a key to Mr. Methven's house and could enter it when he chose to do so. Knowing of the diamonds from Mr. Methven, he did do so the second night after he killed Mr. Methven, his first search after the murder having been unsuccessful. He had not much time then — that is an important point — because Mrs. Raven would be expecting him for the usual drink they had together before lunch almost at once and he had a lot to do, clearing away the signs that he had already had lunch with Mr. Methven. But he took his own key away with him then, so that our attention should not be drawn to how easily he could come and go. And he came back to make that careful, methodical search for the diamonds two nights later, found them, and took them home with him. He and his wife sleep in different rooms, so she would not have known what he was doing."

"Yes, I see," Peter said slowly. "But the murder of Michael Searle, why did that happen?"

"As I have said to you, because he knew too much. He knew from some earlier visit that the key with the red ribbon attached to it belonged to Colonel Raven. He understood what its disappearance meant. And he knew also about the diamonds, which he had been disposing of for Mr. Methven, so he could guess that Colonel Raven had taken them. He threatened him and was killed for his pains. He was a very rash young man. He should never have arranged to meet Colonel Raven alone in Mr. Methven's house last night."

"I don't understand why he should have done that," Peter said.

"But that is quite clear. Colonel Raven is a very arthritic man. He could not have gone to meet Mr. Searle much farther away."

"And Colonel Raven planted Methven's key on him to make it look as if he had done the searching?"

"Of course. It was the obvious thing for him to do."

From the doorway Harriet Raven cried out, "There isn't a word of truth in it. None of it happened. James has never done a dishonest thing in his life."

Sarah had gone up the garden path and was standing beside her godmother. She put an arm round her in a gesture that in her had an unusual look of tenderness, but Harriet shook her off. She did not want comfort just then.

"It's all false, false!" she cried.

Raposo gave a sad shake of his head. "A loyal wife. She will say the same to the end. Now we must go."

He went round the car to get into the seat beside the driver. Behind him James Raven sat stone-faced beside the agente. He did not look at his wife.

"It's false, false!" she cried again.

She ran to the gate and clung to it, shaking it.

Peter put his hand on her shoulder, gently pushing her back from the gate so that he could enter.

"Yes, it's false," he said, "but the question is, are you ready to tell the truth yourself? You've known it all along, haven't you? That's why you cried so over Michael Searle. And I think you may be the only person who can induce Sarah to confess."

CHAPTER 18

Sarah might not have heard him. She stalked into the house and started to go up the stairs.

"Sarah!" Harriet called sharply.

"Tell him to go away," Sarah said. "We don't want him."

"Come in, Mr. Corey," Harriet said. "We've got to talk."

He followed her into the house. She had claimed earlier to be a woman who cried very easily, but now she was dry-eyed.

"I didn't know it all along," she said. "I was afraid of it, but I couldn't have told you why. It was knowing Sarah, I suppose. But I kept hoping I was wrong and I didn't really believe it till I heard the key was missing. Even then I thought it might be James who'd taken it. He's the person I suspected first. But I still don't understand why Sarah killed Alec."

Standing still, halfway up the stairs, Sarah said, "I didn't kill him. I've never thought of killing anyone except myself."

"I know you did it," Harriet said, "but I'd have tried to protect you if you hadn't tried to incriminate James. You shouldn't have put the diamonds in his room."

"I didn't," the girl said. "He didn't say so himself, did he?"

"He was leaving it to me to choose between him and you. If I'd chosen you, I don't think he'd care very much what happened to him."

"Oh, just wait and see. He'll soon be thinking of a way of getting himself out of the mess. He'll come up with some story against me. You know he will. He's always hated me."

"He may have been wiser than I was." Harriet turned to Peter. "Can you tell me why she did it, Mr. Corey?"

"I think I can," he said.

She looked up again at Sarah. "Come down. There's got to be an end to this lying."

"I want to get dressed," Sarah said.

"You can do that presently." Harriet sounded stern, unlike herself. She walked into the sitting room, stood still in the middle of it, and looked round at Peter. "You're going to tell me Michael was her lover, I suppose, the man who left her."

"How long have you known that?" he asked.

"Only since this morning."

There was a sudden flurry of movement behind Peter. Sarah had come racing down the stairs, sped across the hall, and out through the front door.

He would have gone after her if it had not been for Harriet's grip on his arm, the strong grip of a nurse, handling a difficult patient.

"Let her go," she said.

"You know she won't come back."

"If that's how she wants it . . ." She stood still, listening.

They heard the car start up and the sound of it fade as it went up the hill.

Harriet let her breath out in a long sigh.

"I tried, I always tried to do the best I could for her," she said. "but it never seemed to help."

"You can't help people like Sarah," he said. "It's the way they're made."

"Is that what you really believe? That there's no hope for them?"

"Perhaps there was still some hope while she was very young. I don't know about that. But if so, the opportunity was missed."

"That's my fault, then, because there was no one else to help her. Her father loved her deeply, after his fashion, but rather as if she was a young puppy, not a human being. He never really tried to get to know her."

"I don't see why you should blame yourself. You did all you could."

"But I was so wrong, so wrong. James always said I was. He said I was helping to ruin her. But all I did was try to give her some love." She looked round her vaguely as if the room had become unfamiliar to her and she could not think what she was doing there. "I think we should have a drink," she said. But she seemed not to know where drinks were to be found.

Peter went to the dining room, found whisky there, poured out two drinks, and brought them to the living room. Harriet had sat down on the sofa, waiting there stiffly with her feet together, her elbows close to her sides, looking like something very ancient, carved out of marble. Taking the drink that Peter handed to her, she swallowed quickly, then gave a convulsive shudder.

"We must ring the police," she said. "We can't leave James in their hands. But not yet. Give her time. . . . Give her time to do what she chooses. Perhaps after all she'll come back."

"You don't really want her to, do you?"

"That's a terrible thing to say."

"Isn't it true?"

"If I want her dead, I'm the same as she is."

"But you led me in here and you held me back to give her a chance to get out to the car."

"You see too much." She relaxed against the back of the sofa as Peter sat down on a chair facing her. "You do think Michael was her lover, don't you?"

"I thought you'd be able to tell me that," Peter said.

She shook her head. "Not for sure. She never told me who it was, you know. When I tried to get it out of her, she flew into a rage and told me to leave her alone. I suppose it began when they were here two years ago and went on all those walks up in the mountains. But she was such a child, only just sixteen. That's why I never thought about it at the time."

"Sixteen isn't so young nowadays," Peter said. "It's a marriageable age."

"And she killed him for revenge, because of that abortion and then being abandoned by him. But what had she got against Alec? He was always so good to her. He liked young people. The police think James did it to get the diamonds and then killed Michael because he'd found out about it. But Sarah can't have done it for the diamonds. She's got plenty of money of her own."

"I think the diamonds were a blind, and the police have got things the wrong way round. Alec was killed because he knew too much about Michael's murder."

"But it hadn't even happened yet!"

"But when it happened, and she'd already decided it was going to happen, Alec would have known who'd done it."

"Did he knew that Michael had been her lover, then? Did he know about the abortion?"

"I don't think he could have known the whole story, or he'd hardly have encouraged Michael to come here to see her again. But he must have known they'd been in love for a time — either of them might have told him that — and he may have hoped the two young people he cared for would come together again. I think he must have mentioned to Michael that Sarah had come into money, because it was obviously that that brought him. Sarah herself knew that and it must have made her more than ever determined to kill him. Because I think she'd made up her mind before she ever came here that if she ever met him again, she'd do that. It may have been only a kind of fantasy at first, that gradually grew on her the longer she brooded.''

Harriet nodded. ''She said something of the sort to me once, but it was just after her breakdown and of course I didn't take her seriously. She said something about killing the man for what he'd done to her, if she ever met him again. Do you think that was why she stayed on here so long — that she knew he'd come back sooner or later?''

''It may have been. She may even have pressed Alec to persuade him to come.''

''And why she wouldn't tell me who he was. If I'd known, I suppose I'd have guessed at once who killed him. And she thought Alec would have been sure to guess, even if he didn't know everything.''

''There was that, but there were the guns as well. Somehow she knew Alec had three guns. I think he must have shown them to her one day, just to entertain her, and she realised then how she could kill Michael when he arrived. But if Michael had been shot and Alec had discovered that one of his guns was missing, he'd have known at once who'd taken it. So Alec had to be killed first and she went about it quite cold-bloodedly. She went down to the Victoria to swim and had an early lunch at the buffet there, making sure the waiter would remember her, before going up to Alec's house by the back lane and having another lunch with him there. They had omelets, then went out to the patio, I suppose to have coffee. She may have offered to make it so that she could help herself to the gun while Alec was waiting outside. Then she shot him and set about arranging things to look like suicide. Only she's young and ignorant and thought that when she'd done the washing up and removed the eggshells, she'd removed all signs that he'd ever had lunch. She didn't realise that a post-mortem would show up the undigested egg in his stomach. She'd have been wiser, really, to leave the eggshells there, because it's unlikely anyone would have tried fitting them together to see how many eggs had been eaten. And she took the second gun away with her, to be ready to have it to use on Michael; she went back to the Victoria and presently came back here by car, when you expected her. Incidentally, I think that gun went into the sea this morning. She didn't swim, but went down and sat on the rocks by herself. The water's very deep there. It would have been an easy way to get rid of a gun."

"But she was terribly upset by Alec's death," Harriet said. "You saw her yourself. She seemed to go almost out of her mind that evening."

"Yes, and put heavy make-up on her face, to turn it into a kind of mask. It didn't betray much. All the same, though I've never tried it myself, I imagine murder does take it out of you if you aren't used to it. Do you know where she learnt to shoot?"

"She grew up in the country, in Dorset, near to where I lived, and her father used to take her shooting. I expect she knew quite a lot about firearms. But the diamonds . . ." Harriet gulped the rest of her whisky, then put the glass down on a table near her, pushing it away from her, as if to remind herself that she did not intend to have another. "How did she know where they were and why did she take them?"

"I think she knew where they were for the same reason that she knew where the guns were," Peter said. "Alec showed them to her to entertain her. Perhaps he even told her the story of how he got them. And it didn't occur to her to take them when she killed him. She only thought of that when she heard that someone had been searching for something in Alec's house. Someone else — Michael, of course — knew of their existence, but didn't know where they were hidden. And it occurred to her that stealing them would be a perfect cover-up of the real motive for Alec's murder, and she knew she could get into the house any time she chose, because you had his key here. So she took it and let herself in there the following night and removed the diamonds and then carefully rearranged a number of things to make it look as if someone had been searching. She wasn't likely to be suspected for the reason you mentioned, that she's got plenty of money already.

It isn't as if the diamonds had been gem stones, which she might have coveted for their beauty. All they could mean to anyone was money. Then she took the key with the bit of red ribbon tied to it, which she knew was the key to this house, moved the ribbon to the other key, ready to plant on Michael when she killed him, and put your own key where the other had been. And you realised that the keys had been switched and you thought at first, just as she hoped, that your husband must have done it for the very reasons that Raposo thinks so, and you tried to cover up for him, just as he tried to cover up for you, thinking you might have murdered Alec in some mood of jealous anger. I was sure you were both hiding something from the start, particularly you. You looked so frightened."

She did not answer for a moment, but looked at her watch, then seemed unable to withdraw her eyes from it. She might be calculating, Peter thought, how far up the hillside towards the mountains Sarah might have driven by now. Then she gave another deep sigh.

"We'll have to call the police," she said. "We can't leave it too long. . . . D'you know, if she hadn't put those diamonds in his room to incriminate James, because she always hated him so, I might have gone on trying to protect her. I've got so much into the habit of doing it, I'd probably have said nothing about what I guessed."

"If you hadn't, I think that sooner or later there'd have been other murders along the way. Anyone who crossed her would have been in danger. I can't stop thinking about her and Michael yesterday, playing in the sea together. She was almost radiant, yet she knew she was going to kill him that night. She must have been gloriously excited by the thought of it. And she faced him to shoot him, so that he should know what was going to happen to him. When she killed Alec he at least didn't know what she was going to do to him."

"How did she get Michael to meet her in the house?" Harriet asked.

"I think some time in the afternoon, when they were walking in the mountains, she told him she knew about the diamonds and where they were and that she could get the key to the house and let him in. I can't think of anyone else whom he'd have agreed to meet there alone, but he wouldn't have been afraid of her. It was realising that that really convinced me she'd done the murders."

"Well, you'll have to tell all these things to the police." She stood up. "I'm going to telephone them now. But I'm not going to tell them how long we sat here talking."

"No," he agreed.

She left the room and a moment later he heard her talking into the telephone in the dining room.

CHAPTER 19

It was only later that day that it occurred to Peter that for a little while he and Harriet had taken the law into their own hands. They had allowed Sarah to condemn herself. But if they had stopped her taking off for the mountains, it might have turned out that no one would have believed his version of what had happened. She might have gone free and Colonel Raven been sentenced. It was the discovery of her burnt-out car in a ravine in the mountains that settled the matter.

It was found that she had broken her neck before the car caught fire, which gave Peter some sense of relief. To have been burnt alive was worse than anything

327

he could have wished for anybody. But she had died of her own choice and instantly. That it had been Harriet, rather than himself, who had chosen how the girl's story was to end hardly entered his thoughts. In his own mind he was ready to take responsibility for the sentence that had been passed on Sarah.

However, in the long talk that he had with the chefe it did not come out that he and Harriet had sat talking for a considerable time after Sarah had driven away. As Harriet told her own story, this never emerged. It was possible, of course, that even if she had telephoned the police as soon as Sarah left the house, they would have been too late to prevent her from making her final desperate decision. By the time that Harriet had made them understand what had happened and convinced them that they must act, Sarah would have had a long start on them. So Peter's sense of responsibility was to some extent merely the product of an overactive imagination, a peculiar punishment that he inflicted on himself for no good reason.

The police had released Colonel Raven

in the evening of the day on which he had been taken into custody and he had brusquely thanked Peter for his share in clearing him of suspicion. But there had been no more talk of returning to England and Harriet Raven had seemed not to want to see any more of him. Later Peter heard that Sarah had made a will leaving all that she had inherited from her grandaunt to her godmother. Of course, if Sarah had been acquitted or even sentenced to life, the Ravens would not have benefited. When he heard this, Peter did his best to forget the strong grip on his arm that had stopped him from following Sarah out to the car to stop her from driving away.

He spent that evening with Clare, quietly talking over plans for the future adventures of Edward Otter, even though Peter knew that they would never be written. He had at last become clear in his mind about that. When Clare, without saying good-bye to him, left on the early plane the next morning, he realised that they would not see each other again except by accident. And alone, poor Edward had no existence for him.

A few days later, driving out to the airport himself and once more seeing the gigantic, incomprehensible slogans that looked so fierce and dangerous scrawled all over the walls of the pretty gardens, he considered writing one final story in which the savage mink triumphed completely over the peaceful otter. Some savagery in himself made him want to end the story violently. But if he ever did this, he knew, it would simply be a private little tale, written for his own interest and strictly not for publication.